From Ice to Sand

By

Tom Wheeler

Copyright © 2024 Tom Wheeler

ISBN: 978-1-916981-64-5

All rights reserved, including the right to reproduce this book, or portions thereof in any form. No part of this text may be reproduced, transmitted, downloaded, decompiled, reverse engineered, or stored, in any form or introduced into any information storage and retrieval system, in any form or by any means, whether electronic or mechanical without the express written permission of the author.

Chapter 1

Return to the finish.
April 1985.

Bob stood on the on the deck of the MV Kenya returning the waves of Samantha who was on the jetty head ship the Merchant Adventure, she lifted her right hand to her mouth and kissed her fingers and blew the kiss across the water, it hit Bob in the heart like Cupid's Arrow, for the second time in twelve weeks.

Sam Crisp the 28 year old slim five-foot six-inch tall, short dark haired female safety officer from Maidstone in Kent, was waiting to meet Bob English the 34 year old, dark haired, medium height, slim Londoner, who had started the contract as a carpenter but was now workers coordinator, he had been away from the Mount Pleasant airfield project for the past three months, travelling for two weeks to Cape Town in South Africa, four weeks at home, plus four weeks compassionate leave then two weeks returning for a six month extension to the fourteen month contract which he had completed at the end of January.

After the ship transporting the workers had docked and all the formalities of checking and the stamping of passports was complete the passengers were allowed to disembark at which point Bob left the others who were headed to the waiting single decker red buses which would carry them the seven miles to the contractors camp accommodation and went with his suitcases and hand luggage to the waiting Sam who was now sat in the driving seat of a Land Rover that they used together to cover the contract in their duties. After he put his cases and bags in the rear he got in the passenger door, they sat and looked at each other, only to be broken after a few moments by Sam who said, "hello Mr English."

"Hello Miss Crisp," Bob replied, they then started a long passionate kiss. When it was finished Sam said.

"I have missed you so much, I have so much to tell you. I got your letter, I am really so sorry about you and Jane."

"Yeah," Bob rubbed his chin and looked out of the passenger window thinking, he then looked back at Sam and said, "I can't believe it, I thought we were married forever, and then that happened."

"Do you want to talk about it?"

"Yes, but not here."

"That's fine," Sam said as she put the vehicle into gear and they started to move away, "let's go and get something for lunch I've got a single room in the staff block now so we can go back have a cup of tea and a good old natter, how does that sound?" She turned to Bob and smiled.

"Ok, but, well, I am just not the best of company at the moment."

Sam pulled the Rover into one the lay-bys' on the haul road, turned to her passenger and said, "Bob I can't start to imagine how you feel at the moment, but in the time we spent together we both know not only did we become very good friends, but," she smiled at him, "also very close, and I just want to be there for you as a friend, too help you through all of this."

"Thanks Sam, it is just going to take time to get my head around it all."

"And that's," she replied as they moved off again, "fine and I will help you do that."

"Oh, I just don't know what to do," Bob continued, "when these six months are over I think I will just go and join a circus or something."

"Right," came the reply, "so is that a thing you have always wanted to do?" Asked the driver.

Bob laughed.

"Sam I am only joking."

"Oh, you sod, in all the time I have known you I always thought I knew when you were kidding, you caught me out there."

"What," laughed Bob again, "did you think I wanted to be shot out of a cannon?"

"Something like that, you bugger," she thumped him on his right arm with her left fist without looking at him as she drove. They carried on for a while longer then she said, "Kim has said don't worry about seeing anyone about work until tomorrow."

Kim Benjamin was the project coordinator who oversaw the whole contract.

"Blimey he's been here too long if he is starting to be kind!"

"Believe it or not Bob he has also been worried about you. Look let's get something to eat then we can have a good old chat, your back in with Bill with Colin and Ed next door again so we can all get together for the nightly meeting this evening."

"Sounds good to me Miss Crisp.

They headed along the main haul road that went from where the Adventure was moored at West Cove on the East Falkland Islands up April Ridge and on towards the contractor's camp, past the vast rolling green and brown hills and fields. As when he had been away before Bob was amazed with the progress that had been made in the twelve weeks he had been absent from the island.

Permanent road signs had now started to appear as opposed to the temporary wooden ones which had been in place before this, some of which Bob had made in the joiner's shop over the past eighteen or so months, pointing towards the Airfield, Power Station, Compound, Tank Farm, Stanley Road and so on.

"There's something I want to tell you before we get to the camp," Sam put in as it came into sight, "no one knows, it happened while I was on leave."

"Oh, I forgot to ask how the leave went, did you meet someone?"

"Nooo," she pulled over into one of the turning points and turned to face Bob. "No, I haven't met anyone, well I have, and he is sitting beside me," Sam did not give Bob a chance to reply to this. "The leave was good, a nice break, again I did not enjoy the air bridge. Bob, I have been offered a new job."

"Well you have still got five months to go here, you're not jacking, are you?"

"No, let me explain, a chap I worked with for Johnston's for some years got in contact with me, the job is in North Africa, Algeria, they are building, well like big police camps all over the country. His doing the recruiting, he knew I was here and that I speak French, which they talk a lot of there. I had an interview, they are holding it open until I finish. Bob, they want you as well, the two of us, like we are here, moving around the sites, me sorting safety and you like you are doing here, I told them what a great job you are doing, what do you think?"

"Wow, I am not sure what to say, it's a lot to take in, you are not going back to Johnston's after this, you've been there a long time, haven't you?"

"Over ten years, since I was a girl. No, I've liked working for them, and they have looked after me with all the training and everything, but I think it's time for me to move on, this chance may not come along again, and it will be a lot warmer there than here."

"Oh yes, I say so, it will be a bit like from snow to sun, I think anywhere will be warmer than here. The thing is I have now got a divorce to sort out."

"So that's it, I mean you and Jane are finished, it's the end, no way back?"

"Yes, in the extra month off they gave me, I got it all moving, the divorce I mean, and of course the money and everything, I opened a bank account on my own so that she can't get hold of what I don't want to give her. I don't want what happened to Ed, having his bank account cleaned out and being left potless."

"I am really sorry Bob," Sam put her hand on his knee, "do you want to tell me what happened? In your letter you just said you had split up."

"Oh God," Bob took a deep breath, "it was awful. The first week had been fine, then one morning I told Jane to have a lay in bed and I would get the girls breakfast. Karen who is five mentioned Uncle John, I asked who he was, and I am sorry to say I did press her, I had an idea, an old boyfriend of Jane's from years ago, I knew he didn't live far away, then Lynn who's three and a half said, when Uncle John stays he sleeps in Mummy's bed."

"Oh my God." Sam put her hand to her mouth.

"Karen put in, Mummy said not to tell Daddy what we saw."

"Oh Bob, what happened?"

"I went upstairs and woke her up, she did not deny it, then she said things."

"What things?"

"About you."

"ME, what about me?"

"Oh," Bob put his hand on his forehead, and said, "she said she thought me and you were at it, I told her that was not true, but she did not believe me!"

"Well if that's what she thinks, we can soon put that right," said the driver.

"Oh no, I mean not now, not at the moment, oh I would like too, of course, I would but my head is just fucked up at the moment, sorry for swearing Sam, you do mean so much to me, as a friend."

"Did you start smoking again?"

"I did have a few, but I have been off them since I got back on the ship, I really want to stay off them, there's just nothing good about smoking, I see that now. And I will get through this, but one thing is for sure, I don't want to be a smoker at the other side of it"

"Well done."

"Bill has always said any of our wives could be getting done while we're out here, he was bloody right, but I won't tell him that, bloody tosser."

"Oh Bob, I am so sorry."

"Look Sam, along with all this, I have been thinking of you, well apart from needing the money more than ever now, you were the reason I came back, I enjoyed being with you so much."

"Me to, Bob."

"Look Sam, can we be, well, let's just say be boyfriend and girlfriend for a while, and just see how it goes, you know spend time together, go out on our own and things like that?"

"Of course, we can, look Bob, you helped me so much when I first got here. I did feel at one point as if I was in a wilderness, in my mind that is. I had lost my Dad and broke up with Robbie, and I did feel a bit lost, then, well you came along, and we just get on so well together. Now it's my turn to help you."

"Thanks Sam, out of all of this if there is a upside, I will have your help, and." Before Bob could finish, Sam said.

"Bob English, just shut up and kiss me." Sam pulled him towards her by the top of his shirt, and they had another long passionate kiss. When their lips parted, she said, "God I am so pleased to see you, come on, let's go and get some food."

*

"Well I always said that could happen to any of our wives."
"Shut the fuck up Bill," barked Bob, "just shut up."
"Well I am just saying," came the sheepish reply.
"Well don't say," put in Sam. Bob was laying on his bottom bunk in his and Bill's room, the latter was on the top bunk with Colin and Sam sat in the two armchairs facing the bunk beds next to the wash hand basin in the twenty by twenty-foot square room, after they had all had dinner on Bob's first evening back.

"Ok," replied Bill Terry the tall, 34-year-old machine driver with long ginger hair, beard and large dark rimmed spectacles from Birmingham. "I only meant."

"Really, don't mean anything Bill, let's just change the subject," continued Sam.

"Well I heard today," said Colin Watson, the 34-year-old stocky built, fair haired five-foot ten-inch-tall Londoner who had been friends with Bob English since they were young men, "there was a big fight with sackers and jackers last night in the bar next to the video rooms."

"I heard that," said Sam, "there were a couple put in hospital, I believe one of them is in a bad way."

"Well, most of them will be on the next ship then," put in Bob.

"Whose cigarettes are you going to smoke now that Bob's packed them up Bill?" Smiled Sam.

"Don't know Sam, I may have to start buying them."

"Oh," said Bob as he got off his bunk and walked to his wardrobe next to the door, "I nearly forgot, he threw Bill and Colin a pack of two hundred duty free cigarettes each, that's a thanks for sorting the rooms out for us, free of charge."

There came a joint, "thanks," from the pair.

"I've got some for Ed also, where is he, I haven't seen him since we left the ship today?"

"Oh, he is in our room, waiting for someone," said Colin.

"So, have you got any rumours, gossip or stories yet Bob?" Asked Bill as he ripped open his large pack of cigarettes letting the packaging fall to the floor, which Sam bent forward and picked up. He then lit one.

"No, I was given the afternoon off to get sorted, I am meeting with Welfare and then Karl Davis, head of security in the morning, then Kim Benjamin later in the day, I should have lots of news this time tomorrow night."

"I am off then," said Sam, as she got up out of the armchair.

"I'll walk you back, in a few minutes" said Colin, as he went to get out of his armchair.

"Oh, thanks Colin, but won't be necessary, Bob is walking me back, we're boyfriend and girlfriend now, I am buying him a welcome back beer on the way."

"Wow, you kept that to yourself," Colin said to his friend.

"Oh, it's no big deal," he said as he got off his bunk, "it's like Sam said, boyfriend and girlfriend, like being kids again," he smiled.

Before Bob could say anymore the door to the room opened to show Ed, Bob and Sam's driver, a mid thirties-year old, slim and tall man from Newcastle upon Tyne, he was the nephew of George Connors one of the section managers who was very unpopular with a lot of the workforce, he had also come back off leave on the ship that day. "Hi everyone, Colin, there's hmm, someone to see you," he motioned with his head to their room next door.

"Oh, right," he got up, "must go," and without another word he and Ed disappeared.

"Wow," said Bob, "that was all a bit cloak and dagger, one minute he wanted to take Sam home, then in a blink of an eye he was gone."

"Don't worry about him," said Sam, as she held Bob's hand, "come on, you can buy me that drink, see you later Bill."

*

"I am so sorry to hear about your marriage Bob," said Karl Davis, a fifty-three-year-old six-foot-tall ex inspector from the London Metropolitan police and now head of security on the project. "I am still really getting over my own divorce."

"Thanks Karl," Bob sat in the head of security's small windowless office across the desk from him. Metal four draw filing cabinets occupied the remaining areas of the office, which was located in the centre main office complex. "I am still trying to get my head straight, so I am hoping to get on with things here to put it to the back of my mind as much as I can, that is."

"Well Bob, you have come to the right person, I got loads. I would like you to keep your ears to the ground for, never a dull moment here."

"Oh, I will Karl, but I have just been with Joe Benson and he has given me a list of things he wants me to look into also."

"No, I know you will have lots on, but at the same time I know how much you get around, and get to hear things. I have three pressing things I could do with your help on if possible."

"No problem Karl, fire away."

"Do you know Don Brown the section manager?"

"Yes, he hadn't been here long before I went in Jan, he started a section above the airfield, more storage units and offices, I think Section 41?"

"He is still there, one night lately his site was broken into and a digger was used to smash his office up, and whoever did it sprayed painted on the side of the unit in yellow marker paint, 'next time you'll be in it, Brown you tosser.'"

"Bloody hell, I do know he's not top of the hit parade with the lads here."

"There's more, Don was on the radio ordering some concrete the other day when a voice came on and said, 'Brown your life is on the next Kenya,' then the nuts were loosened on his Land Rover. So, this person needs finding Bob, as soon as possible, before he gets Don."

"Ok, I will see what I can find out, what else?"

"Well, we have had, hmm, three rapes."

"Oh my god, are the girls OKAY?" Came the shocked reply.

"It's not girls Bob, it's blokes, men."

"WHAT?"

"Three as far as we know, and I can see some chaps not coming forward over a thing like this."

"Your right, what happened?"

"It seems the same thing every time. They had been having a drink in one of the bars on their own, and each of them were found in a drying room by the night patrol out cold and half naked, trousers off and all."

"Jesus."

"The doc looked at them and said they had been done, you know."

"Up the arse?"

"That's one way of putting it Bob. I think they must have had a drug put in their drinks then taken away as if they were drunk and being taken to their room. Of course, it's with the police, and we have two here all the time now, our little police station has opened while you have been away, it's got two cells', and they have been used, both with drunks. We are keeping the rapes as quite as possible, so we can get him."

"Do you know what Karl, nothing would surprise me here, it's like the old wild west." Bob got up, "I will keep an ear out, got to go, got a meeting to attend."

"There is another thing, well there's loads, but this is what Kim wants sorting as soon as possible, drugs."

"No, I am fine thanks Karl," Bob smiled at his own joke.

Karl did not give an answer to this but carried on, "we have got a drug pusher back, I mean there seems to be loads here again. We got rid of Hack, then his brother Del and that seemed to be the end of it, then after the ship before you came back it all seems it have started again, I've heard there's loads about."

"OK Karl," Bob moved to the door, "will let you know anything I find out, but I must go, see you later."

He left the room with Karl still in his chair. He rubbed his stubbled chin that had not been shaved for the last three days, and said to himself, "I don't think he knows who's selling the drugs this time, unlike before."

*

"What's going on over there?" Sam pointed in front of her, out of the Land Rover window screen as she sat in the middle of Ed who was driving and Bob who was in his usual position next to the passenger door. They had just picked Bob up from his last meeting of the morning with Karl and were heading to the power station, they had left the office compound and were passing the production area where rocks were crushed to make aggregates for concrete, tarmac etc.

Sam was pointing to the large round tall white silo with red letters of the company logo, JLB on the side, that held the cement that went into making the concrete. It looked as if a man was standing on top of the silo, many metres into the air cutting a one-ton bag of cement, open at the bottom which was emptying into the silo, the bag was being held in the air by a crane. "Ed," she continued, "get us over there please, let's see what's going on."

The Land Rover headed towards the batching plant where the operation was being carried out, and parked nearby. Sam walked towards the silo with Bob behind her, both with their white safety helmets on, Ed stood outside the vehicle to smoke a cigarette. Sam waited for the empty bag to swing away from the worker before she called up to him for his attention, Bob had told her his name was Nick Brambly.

"Nick," she called with her hands cupped around her mouth, "can you come down please, I need to talk to you." She had to repeat this a few times before Nick could understand what the safety officer wanted above the noise which was being made around them. Nick came down the cat ladder that was fixed on the outside of the silo, when he got to the ground the short stocky built, fair haired man who was covered in cement from Coventry, walked over to them and said,

"What is it? I am very busy you know."

"What are you standing on up there?" Asked Sam.

"Scaffold boards."

"Just boards?" Asked Bob

"Two side by side and they are doubled up."

"That's not safe," continued the safety officer, "you must not go back up there until I or Tom Smith have inspected it and say it is safe to do so."

"I take my orders from my foreman, Andy York."

"No, if it's a safety issue, you take your orders from Tom or I."

"Well," pointing behind them, "you had better tell him then," from a small office at the other side of the compound and now marching towards them was the foreman, a not very tall and overweight person in his fifties from Norwich in Norfolk.

"What's going on here?" Asked the angry looking foreman.

"Good morning Andy," Sam put her hand out to shake hands with the newcomer, who shook it. "We met a couple of months ago at a staff meeting, Sam Crisp."

"Oh yes, I remember, morning Bob, what's going on here, why have you stopped this man from working?"

"It's too dangerous for Nick to work up there," replied Sam.

"We have no choice, the pump that gets the cement into the silo has broken and needs a new one which has only just been ordered, and as a cargo ship has just left the UK it will be on the one after that, which is about seven or eight weeks away, so he has to carry on, and we are paying him double time when he is up there."

"Well he could fall off or into the silo, with the bag swinging or by the wind, which never seems to stop blowing here, he also needs the correct protective clothing and a mask on, and until that all happens I will not let him go back there."

"Do you know what love," barked the now very angry foreman, "you can go fuck yourself!"

"Well if it's okay with you, I am hoping I will have Bob doing that for me soon," at this point Bob's mouth dropped open, "so if we can put my private life to one side? I want a scaffold tower put up there so Nick can stand on the top safely, with a safety harness on, the yellow plastic overalls, a safety helmet, gloves, goggles and mask, or do you want me to get Kim Benjamin," she held her radio in the air, "over here to tell you to do it?"

"Hmm, well that won't be necessary, but we need cement in the silo."

"How much is there in it at the moment Nick?" Asked the safety officer.

"Oh, it's almost full," said the cement covered worker, "am I going to lose my double time when this is all in place?"

"No," she continued, "it's still not a nice job, in fact it's horrible. I will make sure you still get paid double time while it's going on, and if there is a problem come and see me or Bob. As the silo is full Andy, I suggest you get on the radio now to the scaffold foreman, tell him it's an urgent safety issue, if he has a problem at all tell him to call me. We will be back this way in an hour or so to see how it's all going, see you later, come on Bob, and you can close your mouth now!"

*

"What news have you got for us," asked Bill from his top bunk as he laid smoking at the nightly meeting, "and where's your girlfriend tonight?"

"Oh, she's washing her hair," came the reply from the committee man, who was making tea for those two plus Colin and Ed who were sitting in the armchairs, "we are going to see a video later."

"Well if I was going out with her," put in Colin, "I'd be over there every night, at it, in fact I would move in with her."

"Well firstly," said Bob as he handed the plastic yellow tea cups out, "you're not going out with her."

"She wouldn't have you," smiled Bill from above.

"And secondly," he continued as he sat on his bunk, "it's not like that, I have just broken up with Jane, and it is, well it's just nice going out with her, better than being with you smelly lot every night," he laughed.

"She has changed you already, after a few months," put in Colin.

"HOW? She hasn't."

"She made you pack up smoking," continued his ex-roommate.

"Oh, I wanted to do that for years, you know that, it costs a fortune, and is no good for you. You lot could do with doing the same."

"You don't swear when she's about," put in Ed.

"Fuck off!" Came the smiling reply.

"Come on," Bill said, "before you go out give us some news."

"Well there's dope being sold here again, it seems there's loads about at the moment, Karl has asked me to keep an ear out, they are mad to find them and get them off the island." This news was greeted by complete silence in the room, which did not go unnoticed by Bob. "Have I said something?"

"I told you," said Ed.

"Shut the fuck up," snapped Colin.

"Please don't," Bob stood up, "tell me it's you," looking at the pair in the armchairs.

"I only brought it back, I am not selling it," Ed spat out.

"Me too," said the voice from the top bunk behind Bob.

"SHUT UP," snarled Colin.

"OH FUCK," Bob sat on his bunk again, "are you mad, you'll all be sacked."

"I haven't got any in here," put in Bill, "it's all next door," he pointed to the others room.

"I haven't got it in my wardrobe, it's in his," put in Ed as he pointed to his roommate.

"Oh, THANKS, lads," snapped Colin.

"Well it was your idea," said Bill, "you paid us two to bring it back."

"Oh fuck," said Bob, "my best mates here are international drug smugglers." This brought a round of laughter from the others. "It's not fucking funny," he stood up, "you'll all get sacked, and criminal records into the bargain, you're fucking MAD!"

"Calm down Bob," Colin stood up, "we can make a fortune here, it's one of the reasons I came back, I've got a load coming on the next Kenya, I didn't want you to know, I knew you wouldn't be happy, you're not going to say anything, are you, mate?"

"No, of course not," he walked across the room and picked his jacket off the hook on the back of the door, "no I won't, but I still think your all fucking MAD!" He turned and left the room slamming the door behind him.

*

A few nights after Bob's row with the lads regarding the drugs, Ed was sat at a table on his own in the large bar which was now known as the New Gull & Penguin. He was on his second pint of the evening, it was a Wednesday night around nine fifteen. It was quiet in the bar with it being mid-week, Ed had just returned from the lavatory and was carrying on reading the local Newcastle newspapers that his mother sent him out most weeks. He had taken a few more mouthfuls of his beer when he started to feel dizzy. He was not sure what to do as he tried to call out for help but he found he could not, he was about to fall off his chair when he was grabbed from behind under the armpits and his slim frame was lifted into the air on to his feet.

"Come on old chap," said the west country of England accent from behind him, that was the last thing Ed remembered. "I'll get you home lad," said the large framed six foot two, bearded face worker who held him up then marched him out of the bar with one on Ed's arms over his shoulder, past the video rooms and telephones towards the exit, telling anyone who might have cared that, "he's had too much, I'll get the lad home." Ed was led along the floodlit pathways outside into the dark and becoming cold May evening in this southern part of the world, towards the large accommodation block. He was not taken into the first drying room but the one at the start of the 'D' corridor. Ed's kidnapper looked around him before opening the door, then turned the lights off, so only the emergency light was on over the door. He then dragged Ed behind the centre locker cages and dropped him to the floor, "right my beauty," he smiled to the unconscious body that lay before him on the floor, "you're a lovely looking lad." Before anything else could happen, the door swung open and the room was illuminated, Karl, Bob and a security guard appeared around the cages to confront Ed's assailant who had been watching them since the "set up" in the bar.

"Right," said Karl, "game over, it's time to come with us, cuff him Billy."

Billy the medium height mid forty's Scottish security guard walked towards the, now very angry looking, would be rapist, and said, "put your hands out lad." He looked at Billy and as he got closer to him and said.

"Fuck off," he then pulled his head back and head-butted Billy in the face causing him to crash to the floor, he then rushed forward and pushed Karl backwards who fell in turn onto Bob for the two of them to fall to the floor. The attacker run to the door and opened it to disappear into the corridors to make his escape, only to be met by a size ten steel toe capped boot that was on the end of Bill Terry's right leg, it swung up with as much force as it owner could muster and crashed between the top of his legs, he held his testicles with both hands as he fell to his knees before passing out. Bill was joined in the corridor by Karl and Bob, as he said, "take that you arse raping bastard!"

*

"I think you were really lucky Ed," said Sam as she sat on a chair next to Bob on the left-hand side of Ed's hospital bed with Karl on the opposite side in the otherwise empty four bed ward the next morning. "I mean you could have been killed by those drugs he gave you, and you two set it up, and more to the point you said nothing to me."

"Because you would have said no," replied Bob. Before the female could reply, Karl put in.

"Sam, we had to stop this, hmm bloke, or I think he would have killed someone in the end, I don't think he was about to stop. When we went into his room he had a bag full of the drug capsules in his wardrobe. And it was all set up for the medics to treat Ed."

"And I was up for stopping him," said Ed, he held his forehead, "mind you, I have got the worst headache that I can ever remember having in my whole life."

"And you did get overtime paid at double time and your beer paid for, for the last three nights," Bob pointed out.

"Well there is that," replied the man in the bed.

"So that's where you have been all week," said Sam, "and you said you were helping Karl sort some problems," before anyone could say anything she answered her own question by saying, "I supposed that's what you've done."

"Look Sam," Karl continued, "this chap is now out of here, he is locked up in Stanley and will soon be back in the UK."

"What will he be charged with," asked Bob.

"Well, I am not really sure, I have never come across male rape before, the lads in the UK have said they are going to look up the case law on it. Look I have got to go," said Karl as he got up, "well done Ed," he shook his hand, "Kim is pleased we have got him, and he said to have two days off with pay, I've got to go. See you all later," he turned and left the ward.

"Bloody hell," said Bob, "Kim is really going soft in his old age."

"I could have been killed, like Sam said, mind you I never really thought of that."

"You just thought of the free beer and double overtime, so don't rip the arse it," smiled Bob as he got up, "have a rest mate," he shook his hand, "Sam can do the driving."

"Oh thanks," she got up, "mind you I have heard about your driving Bob English," she leant over and kissed Ed on the cheek, "take care Ed, we'll see you soon." They turned and left the ward. As they walked towards their Land Rover that was parked outside the medical centre, Bob pulled Sam back by the arm and said.

"Sam, I am really sorry for not telling you what we were doing, but he had to be caught and I didn't want to put you on the spot, health and safety wise, if you knew."

The female safety officer looked at him and after a short while of thinking said, "I do understand it all, and you all had the best intention, he had to be stopped, and I will forgive you, if we bunk off work for an hour or so and you take me to see the penguins at Westland Beach, I've got something for you."

"It's a deal Miss Crisp, I can't wait."

*

"It's turning cold," said Sam as she sat on a sand dune with her blue rain proof jacket zipped up to her chin, and a black woollen hat pulled over her ears. She was half laying on Bob who had his left arm around her shoulders, they were on Westland Beach, in front of them was a Rock Hopper penguin rookery which in turn was in front of the choppy, cold South Atlantic Ocean.

"Yes," he replied to his girlfriend, "winter is on its way, cor blimey, there was lots of snow and really cold last year, they said it was the coldest winter here for almost forty-five years. Those penguins are so noisy and really pen and ink when the wind blows this way," Bob mockingly held his nose.

"How come Bill was in the corridor, when it all happened?"

"Me and him had a radio in our room the nights we were doing it, Billy the security guard was working collecting glasses and keeping an eye on Ed, Karl was in the next bar with a radio. We all got paid overtime while it was going on."

"I must say you worked it all out, I am pleased you got him."

"Yes, one less nutter here, only two thousand left," he smiled, "you said you have something for me, what is it?"

"Oh yes," she sat up, unzipped her jacket and pulled out of the inside pocket a white envelope, with Mr Bob English typed on the front, "the postman has come, a letter for you Mr English, sir," she handed it to him.

"Oh," said Bob in a surprised voice, as he took it and started to open the letter, "it's not your handwriting," he joked as he took the folded paper out, and opened it to see the name Kingston & Easton on the top, then started to read to himself, when he was finish he said, "oh wow, you know what this is, don't you?"

"Yes, it was in with my contract offer for Algeria, I only got it last night, and of course I have not seen you to talk to, not with the Ed thing and everything, what do you think?"

"This is really all happening very fast, I haven't had time to think."

"That's how life is at times Bob, you can't stand still."

"I know Sam, but I have had so much happen of late," he looked at the penguins running in and out of the cold sea, coming back with fish to feed the young chicks on, for a short while, then turned to Sam and said, "you're really up for this job in Algeria, aren't you?"

"I am, I have been thinking about it, a lot. Being here has got me going, it's given me the travelling bug, working with lads who have worked around the globe, I would really like to go and work in other places in the world Bob. After fourteen months I will be ready to move on from here, but I would really, really, really like to do it with you. I think we make a really good team, what do you think?"

He looked at the sea again for a few moments, then turned and held Sam in both arms and said, "the money they are offering is more than I am on here, and of course all tax-free again, and I could do with the money now more than ever, and we would be moving all around the country, it does sound good." He thought for a moment, then continued, "we can't tell anyone until a month or so to go here."

"I have thought about that, I will come up with some reason to extend my contract for an extra month here, so we can both leave together, and be on the Kenya on our own for two weeks, don't forget I have never done that trip. I can get us in the same cabin, we then have a month off, stay at my place in Maidstone, we then take your girls away on holiday, somewhere hot for two weeks, then it's off to North Africa, and lots of sunshine and more tax-free money. All only an idea that is, and if you are okay with it?"

Bob sat thinking for a moment, then said, "you have really thought this through, haven't you Miss Crisp?"

"Of course, Mr English, I am a woman, now shut up and kiss me!"

Chapter 2

We'll Smoke to That!

Winter had commenced and at the beginning of June 1985, snow had been falling most days on and off, not so much as it was causing major problems with the project but with the temperature being around zero most days and the wind blowing from the south, the conditions were not very pleasant for those working outside.

A large amount of the permanent roads had been laid but a lot of the temporary haul roads that would disappear at the end of the project were again cutting up profusely with continued use by heavy vehicles and the damp conditions.

The gang which was tasked with maintaining and keeping them open had been nicknamed by the lads as West Cove County Council. Their gangerman was a fifty-six-year-old from North Devon, Del Parker. He had always appeared to be on the strange side, mainly because of some unusual comments he would make from time to time, but of late appeared to have worsened. Bob had been asked by Welfare to have a word with him.

There was still a lot of work to complete in and around the airfield, but now it was operational many work hours had to be changed to accommodate flights. Bob had been asked to help with the coordination of this. Work which had not been vital to the first landing had now commenced.

While work on the RAF accommodation had progressed well, construction had also commenced on other facilities in this location which in time would include, a library, education centre, gym, swimming pool, kart racing track, climbing wall, hairdressers, two NAAFI shops, (Navy, Army and Air Force Institutes) medical centre, there was also plans for a golf cause and talk of sometime in the future, the islands first cricket pitch.

*

"Sam, can I come to your room after work tonight?" Bob asked his co-worker as they sat in the Land Rover waiting for Ed to return from picking up doggie bags for their lunch at the power station canteen.

"Oh Mr English, this sounds very interesting," Sam smiled.

"Sam, it's not like that, I need to talk to you, on our own, hmm, I mean, you and me, like private."

"Sorry, Bob, I was kidding, you sound serious."

"Yes, I have a couple of things I need, me and you, hmm, you and I to talk over, you are the only person I have here to do that with," he turned and looked out of the front window, "oh shit Ed's here."

"In my room at eight," the information was given just before the driver's door opened.

*

"Hi Del, how's it going?" Bob asked the road maintenance ganger as they stood beside the small road scraper that Del occasionally operated when he was not giving instruction to his workforce, this was parked in one of the haul roads turning points.

"Not bad Bob lad, busy as ever."

"You and the lads have done a great job keeping the roads open."

"Yeah, tosser's up in the office," he pointed forwards, "would never give us any extra money, tight bastards."

"I know Del, we have mentioned it at the meetings, but you have done well out of the overtime."

"Yeah, I know, what do you think of the dog then?" The gangerman pointed near the tracks of the machine which had nothing there. "He's grand, isn't he? A Golden Labrador, brought him off one of the Bennies at the weekend, got to go Bob, can't be talking here all day," he climbed up on the open-top machine and started it up as Bob was looking for the invisible dog. "Come on Dodger," he shouted above the noise as he put a pair of ear-defenders on, "I call him Dodger because he dodges between all the machines, see you later Bob, come on boy." Del pulled away leaving the committeeman in the lay-by looking around himself.

20

Whilst doing this his Land Rover pulled up with his two co-workers to collect him, with Sam looking out of the open passenger window, she asked.

"What are you looking for?"

"The dog." He continued looking.

"What dog."

"Del's dog, the Golden Labrador, Dodger."

"There's no dog here Bob."

"He's barking," he replied as he made for the vehicle.

"Barking, the dogs barking, I can't hear him."

"Nooo, Del."

"Why was Del barking?" Asked a now very puzzled safety officer.

"Nooo," came the reply as he opened the door and started to get in. "Del's barking, he's barking bloody mad, with an imaginary dog."

"And what's even more worrying Mr English," she smiled, "is that you were looking for the dog."

*

"Thanks Sam, it makes a change having tea made for me," Bob said as he received the cup off Sam as he sat in the armchair next to the one she then sat in.

"No problem, so what do you want to talk about, it all sounded very serious."

"I am not sure how to start this, hmm, well, it's drugs."

"How do you mean?"

"I know who's supplying them, and who brought them in."

"Well," came the reply, "you know you have to report them, don't you?"

"Aha, it's not that easy."

"Tell me who it is and I will tell Karl, I don't have a problem with that," continued Sam.

"This has really put me on the spot, Colin is selling them and Bill and Ed also brought stuff in for him."

"Nooo, are you sure?"

"Oh yes, Ed tripped up and told me, I promised I wouldn't say anything, I can't rat on them, but I want to get it stopped before they get caught and lose their jobs, and all their outstanding monies, and of course get a criminal record into the bargain."

"Hell, look Bob, you know how I feel about this sort of thing."

"Please don't tell on them."

"No, I will not, not because of them, no it's because of you, you confided in me, and I can see how this has put you in a difficult position."Sam took a sip of tea, then continued, "I will help you, but you're right it's got to stop."

"Yes, you're right, but without dropping them in it, I don't know how, he's got a load coming on the next Kenya." They sat for a few moments drinking their teas when Sam said.

"I have got it; do you know who brings it in?"

"I think it's a crew member from The Kenya, they call him Chinese John, I don't know his surname."

"There can't be many Chinese John's on the ship," smiled Sam.

"No," laughed Bob, "I think it's him anyway, he used to supply Hack and his brother Del. Oh, do you know what? I saw Ed talking to him one night outside the bar just before we got back, of course, I didn't put two and two together, you idiot," he hit his own forehead with the palm of his right hand.

"Right, you go and see Karl, The Kenya is back in a few days."

"Yes, it is, Wolfie and Reg are on it, I can't believe I have been back here almost a month."

"You tell Karl who is going to bring the drugs in, not who he is selling them to."

"The ship's crew are allowed to come up to the camps duty free shop, that's when they will meet, I bet," replied Bob.

"We stop the drugs coming in, they can't sell them, job done," smiled Sam.

"Your brilliant Miss Crisp."

"Ok," came the reply, "what's next, you said you had a couple of things to talk about, we are on a roll?" She smiled.

"Well, on top of all of that, I had a letter from Jane last night."

"Okay," came the cautious reply.

"She has said she is really sorry, and wants to get back together and start again."

"Oh, so right, hmm, what do you think, are you going to?"

"No way, I have sent her a very long letter back, I stayed up late writing it and posted it tonight, and aha, told her in not so many words, hmm, to go and get fucked, sorry Sam. I could never trust her again after what happened, and this letter has really messed with my head, and it's not as if she hadn't done so already."

"Right." As she spoke the female safety officer held his hand.

"When I went home I just didn't know what to do about coming back, and I have got to say I think I was leaning towards staying at home, because I didn't want to mess with your head, and mine, then BANG! I get hit with the bombshell."

"Sometimes things happen for a reason Bob."

"Yeah, I know, you can say that again. No, there's no way back Sam, it's over."

"I am so pleased, not that you have broken up," she took her time then looked him in the face and said, "Bob this may make me look a fool, but I am going to say it anyway. I love you so much," Bob went to talk but Sam put her fingers on his lips, "please just let me finish, I need to say this, and now is the time," she took a deep breath. "Bob, I have never felt like this for anyone, like I do about you at this moment. While you were on leave I was broken up, and it's not right I know, but when you said you and Jane had split up, well, I was just over the moon." Bob went to talk, but again Sam stopped him. "Bob, Bob English I just love you so much, I just want to be with you, we are just so good together, I just feel so good, happy when we are with each other. Had you not have come back, and I was preparing myself for that, as I knew you would have been loyal to Jane, then what happened, happened." She squeezed his hand. "Now you may talk sir."

"Wow," Bob blew a breath out, "that's a lot to take in, but, hmm, well, as you know my head has been really messed up, but you have been really helping me, and well the truth is, I feel the same for you." Before he could say anymore, once again she stopped him and said.

"Bob that is all I wanted to know, now I know I have joked about us having sex, don't say a word, that was all a joke, because I really want you, I don't want sex, I want us to make love, because Mr English, I love you so much, please come with me." They both stood up and hand in hand walked towards Sam's bed.

*

"Thanks for seeing me at short notice Karl, I have been trying to see you for the past couple of days, then I found out you were away," said Bob as he sat in Karl's small office.

"Oh, I have been away in the capital, doing some training which I was told I had to do, just got back, have to be here for the Kenya docking." He looked at his wrist watch, "in fact I have to go very soon as I have to be there for the dismemberment."

"That's what I have come to see you about, I know who's bringing the drugs onto the island."

"Oh Bob, that's great news, who is it?"

"He is a crew member, I don't know his surname, but they call him Chinese John."

"Oh, that won't be a problem, I have loads of informers on the ship, so who's he selling to?"

"Oh, aha, I don't know that, I was only given that name, you can just pick him up when he leaves the ship to come up to the camp shop."

"So that's where they are meeting is it, at the camp shop?"

"Hmm, I didn't say that." Bob shifted in his seat in a nervous manner.

"Well I think you did, are you sure you don't know who he is selling to Bob?"

"Nooo, no, not at all, they all come up to the shop, I just guessed at it, look Karl, just pick up this John, and it's sorted, he gets arrested and sacked and you have stopped the drugs coming in, none of the other crew will chance it after that, and Kim will be really pleased with you."

"No, I want the one selling it as well, the dealer, I will have John followed and when he meets his buyer, we'll get them both."

"I thought you would be pleased to get the supplier off the ship, and have it stopped coming in."

"Bob, once a copper always a copper, I want as many nicking's as possible, and that will send out a real scare message to anyone else thinking of doing it in the future."

"Right," the visitor said, as he got up, "I've got to go."

"Well thanks for the info Bob, I will let you know how it goes."

"No problem," said Bob as he hurried out of the office. Karl sat in his office and rubbed his chin and said, "he knows who's buying it alright," as he picked up the telephone on his desk.

*

Sam and Ed were waiting in the Land Rover outside of the offices for Bob, he ran to the vehicle, once inside he said, "Ed, get us over to the camp shop asap, they know there's a drugs deal going down, they know it's Chinese John and they are going to pick him up and the person he sells it to, Colin."

"Oh shit," said Ed, as he drove off.

"What's all this?" Asked Sam, as if she knew nothing about it.

"Oh, aha, there's something I have to sort out, I will explain it all to you later."

"Okay." She replied.

The roads were full of traffic, more than normal with the ship being in, they got stuck behind two buses who were making their way from the compound to the camp to pick up those going on the ship.

Karl had been busy since Bob left, he had rung the ship and now knew Chinese John, was John Simpson from Dover in Kent, he had been told that he had already left with the rest of the crew for the shop, he then rang his men at the camp and a welcoming committee would be waiting for John and his buyer.

When Bob and co got to the shop the crew bus was already there, but looking around he could not see Colin, he had seen John who had a large bag over his shoulder sitting on a bench near the shop. Bob had walked back to the parking area behind the shop when he saw Colin pull up, as fast as he could he raced to the vehicle and got in the passenger seat next to a very surprised Colin.

"Hi Bob, what are you doing here?"

An almost out of breath Bob said, "saving you, again I may add."

"What?"

"I have been in with Karl Davis this morning and he said he had to go as they were about to go and arrest Chinese John who they know is bringing drugs on to the island and they were also going to get the person he is selling to, they had been given info from someone on the ship."

"Piss off, you're just saying that so I don't buy them, nice try Bob, but I have known you too long." He made to get out of the vehicle.

"COLIN, this is no wind up, believe me, if you walk around that corner and meet John you will be sat in a police cell tonight, with no job, a criminal record and lost all the money they are holding on you, you'll lose everything."

"Bob, I don't believe you."

Bob shook his head and said, "FINE!" Then opened the door, "we have been mates' a long time, but I have now given up trying to help you, GO, then when I see you at home next, I can say I told you FUCKING SO!" He barked at his friend, almost spitting in his face.

Colin took a cigarette out and lit it and said, "you're not kidding, are you?"

"Nooo, you have done some stupid things here, but we are still mates', look my marriage has gone, yours could go too when Jean finds out about all of this, just think. I really am telling you the truth, believe me, walk around that corner and your life will be changed forever! Just turn around and go back to work."

After thinking for a few moments, Colin put his hand out to his friend and said, "okay, thanks Bob, again, you are a real mate."

"Just get out of here in case John rats on you, if you're not around you can just deny it." He then got out of the Land Rover and returned to his, which was waiting at the other side of the large car park with his two co-workers in.

It was after the ship had left that Karl called Bob on the radio and asked him to pop into his office as soon as he could.

"We got Chinese John," said Karl as Bob sat down in his office.

"Well done, don't let on to anyone it was me who told you."

"Of course not, but we didn't get who he was selling it to, the crew were about to return to the ship so we had to pick John up on his own."

"Oh, that's a shame," replied Bob meaningfully.

"Yeah, John is over in the capital now, in court tomorrow, then back to the UK on a ship taking soldiers back the next day. He had loads on him."

"Good," said Bob, as he started to get up.

"We asked him who he was selling to."

"Right, aha, what did he say?"

"Said he only knew him as Col, I think that's short for Colin?"

"Could be."

"You've got a friend named Colin here, haven't you, the one who was involved in selling scrap metal that time?"

"Bloody hell Karl," he snapped, "how many Colin's must there be here?"

"A lot I would say, well there is in fact eight, I checked."

"So, it could have been any of those eight, I am off Karl." Bob turned to leave.

"It would have been nice to have got the pusher as well Bob."

"Yes, it would have Karl, but guess WHAT?" Barked Bob.

"What?"

"You have stopped the drugs getting onto the island, here anyway, that has got to make it a good day for you?"

"Oh, it does Bob, it really does, and please don't misunderstand how much I value and appreciate how you help me, and thank you again Bob." He held his hand out across the desk to shake, which the committeeman looked at then shook, as he told himself.

'Get out of here now Bob English.' "No problem Karl, see you later," he turned and left the office.

Karl rubbed his chin and said, "I hope Colin Watson knows how much his mate looks after him?"

*

"Welcome back Wolfie, Reg, good to see you both," smiled Bob. There were handshakes all around with the returning workers who had all met in the bar for a drink the evening they had arrived back.

Bill, Colin, Sam and Ed were also there as they took their places at the large round table, Sam kissed them both on their cheeks when she returned from the bar with Ed after buying everyone a drink. The bar was getting full and noisy as they always did on the night a ship came in.

"Cheers Sam," plastic glasses were held in the air to thank their friend, the safety officer, for the beers.

"Well lads, what have we missed since we have been away?" Asked Wolfie, the tall, long grey haired, bearded fifty-year-old from County Durham.

"Nearly every night there is no hot water," said Colin, "if you get in late from work you have no chance of a hot shower."

"I've got it on the list for our next committee meeting, it's the day after tomorrow Reg." He nodded his agreement as he took a sip of beer. Reg from Derby, was well built, in his late forties, had come out as a machine driver, but was also Bob's fellow committee member.

"Put on your list about the shower heads going missing," put in Bill.

"I will, but what's all that about?" Asked the committee chairman.

"You really don't know do you," smiled Sam, "well you are men," she mocked.

"What?" Asked Ed.

"It's the girls, women, they put bits of hose pipes on them and they can then wash their hair in their rooms' in their wash hand basins."

"You are joking," said Colin.

"No joke, I brought one when I was at home, but I know a lot of the girls have done it."

"That's got to be a health and safety issue?" Asked Ed.

"I'll let your trusted committee deal with that one," smiled the safety officer.

"I heard one of the ship's crew got picked up today," put in Reg, "had a big load of dope on him, and was about to sell it to someone, I don't think they got the buyer."

"No," commented Bob, "I did hear he got away, must have done a runner when he saw security there!"

"I heard," said Bill quickly changing the subject, "that one of Eastham's girls went on today's ship, with a belly full of arms and legs, and the two twins who were on the game both got sacked, I am told one of them had the clap."

"No surprise there, about the clap that is or the belly full for that matter," put in Wolfie.

"A belly full of arms and legs?" Asked Sam.

"With child," said Bob who was sitting next to her, "she's having a baby."

"OH!"

"How was your leave Wolfie?" Asked Colin.

"Oh, not that good really, fell out with the wife."

"Again?" Put in Bob.

"Yeah, we had agreed I was going to redo the kitchen while I was home, she was going to stay at her cousins while I did it."

"The one you don't get on with?" Asked Bill.

"That's her," he made a pretend spit on the floor, which brought smiles from all in attendance around the table. "Well before she went, the wife that is, we could not agree how to do it, she wanted to do the walls in tiles, I wanted to do them in wood. Well we had a real old ding-dong over it all."

"What did you do?" Asked Sam.

"Well, she was away with the kids, so I did two walls in tiles and two walls in wood."

"Nooo," Replied the female in the next but one seat to him, "what did she say when she saw it?"

"She went mad, said I was to change it, I said I would, when I come home next time."

"And you're still married? Asked Sam.

"Well, we are at the moment, mind you I have been at sea for two weeks, so who knows what will be in the next letter," he laughed. "Anyway, while I was at home I heard some massive projects are starting or ongoing in the world that are taking on ex-pat British workers."

"Where are they?" Asked Reg.

"There is a massive dam coming up in China, but I think that may be a few years off yet." He took a drink of his beer, then continued, "there are two big jobs started in North Africa."

"Whereabouts?" Asked Sam.

"There is a really big water treatment plant in Egypt, just outside Al Qahirah."

"Where's that?" asked Bill.

"Better known as Cairo," put in Sam.

"Who's a clever girl," smiled Wolfie.

"That's very impressive, Miss Crisp," smiled Bob.

"So, where's the other one?" Asked Sam.

"Oh," Wolfie continued, "that's in Algeria, of course also North Africa," Sam was holding Bob's hand under the table, and gave it a gentle squeeze. "I believe that work is all over the country, even goes down to the Sahara Desert. They are called gendarmeries, they are like large headquarters, or barracks for the gendarmes there."

"I believe Algeria is the second largest country in Africa, after Sudan. Are you putting in for any Wolfie?" Asked Sam.

"You are a clever girl," the female smiled at the comment. "I have put in for both in North Africa, worked in Africa a few times in the past, might do one of them after this and then maybe on to the one in China if it's started."

"Will you ever work at home again?" Asked Bill.

"Not if I can help it lad, I don't like the horrible thing they ask you to do there, pay income tax." The gathered drinkers all laughed at the comment.

Sam stood up, "your wife may have forgiven you over the kitchen by time you finish in North Africa," she smiled, "I am going to the ladies," she said to Bob then bent and kissed him on the forehead. She moved around the table towards the lavatories, in doing so she had to pass a group of rowdy drunken workers, one of them stood in her way and said.

"What are you doing with that lot love, come and join us," he made a move for her upper left arm area, before he could touch her she grabbed his right wrist with her right hand, twisted it, turned him around put his arm up his back and pushed him into his mates who all laughed at him and said.

"Not tonight darling," both Bob and Bill had got up, but she just said, "it's fine lads, just had too much to drink, see you soon."

"Wow," said Wolfie, "she is going to make someone a great wife one day!"

Chapter 3

Look into the fish pond.

Bob was sitting in Doctor Death's office, "well Bob, we have your results," he looked at the file in front of him, "you have three weeks to live." Bob sat in shock, "we will send you home on The Kenya next week to be with your family."

"Can't I go Air Bridge?"

"No, I can only send people Air Bridge if it's an emergency."

"Is this not a fucking emergency?" Bob snapped.

"No need to swear old chap, no it is not really an emergency, going home early will not save you, the truth is you will properly die on The Kenya anyway, but it's not a problem, we can fly your body home from South Africa, that's not a problem at all old chap."

"I think I am going to be sick," he stood up from the chair.

"Oh, can you go outside and do it please, NURSE," the doctor called out, the door opened at immediately, "can you get a bowl please, Bobs going to be sick." One appeared in her hands as if by magic, just in time for Bob to cough a large amount of blood into it, this was then followed by a lung, then a kidney, then his heart, he fell to the floor, the doctor and nurse looked down on him and the doctor said, "he doesn't look very good nurse!"

Bob woke up in his bunk sweating, below Bill who was snoring heavily, "oh shit, what was that all about?"

*

"Come in Tom Smith or Sam Crisp please," the radio said as Sam, Bob and Ed headed away from the Tank Farm in their Land Rover.

"Sam here." The female spoke into the handset.

"Hi Sam, Jason Hardwick here, up on the drainage dig west of the airfield."

"Yes, I know where you are Jason, how can I help?"

"Is it possible to get over here, hmm, there's something I think you need to look at."

"Ok, we are on our way."

They headed to the drainage dig which was taking the main storm/surface water away from the runway. While the drains at each side of the runway were working they were running into a very large pit/soak-away, as a temporary measure until the main drains at the end of the runway were in place. Until that was complete there was always the chance of areas of the runway flooding. The pressure was on for this work to be completed. Again, they had hit a large amount of rock and had started blasting to make progress.

"Jelly, it's fucking jelly," said Ed as the three new arrivals looked into the trench with Jason.

"I've cleared the area," the thirty-four-year-old Jason said.

"Good, we will have to stop work until this is sorted," before she could continue talking Tom Smith's Land Rover pulled up behind them, he then joined them at the trench. "It's unexploded gelignite Tom, we are going to have to stop this blasting, it's just too dangerous," Sam told the newcomer.

"I've just come from talking to Kim about it, he says we can't stop, it's too important, it's got to keep going."

"You are joking, someone is going to get killed, I wasn't here but I know what happened last year, and that was pure luck no one died," Sam said with anger in her voice.

"It's what I have been told Sam."

"Right, you and I, let's go and see him now."

"Okay, come in my Land Rover."

"Sam, can I just have a minute please," Bob led her away by her left elbow without waiting for an answer. When they were out of ear shot from everyone Bob said, "Sam, don't let Kim upset you, you are on the run down to leaving here and going to Algeria, don't tell him to poke it, as jacking and breaking your contract will do your work record no good at all."

"I promises to stay calm, it's nearly knocking off time, I will come around to you tonight, to tell you what happened and I will bring my dream book so we can try to work out your dream from last night, see you later darling," she turned and walked to the waiting Land Rover.

*

"A watcher?" Sam replied to Tom Smith, whom she was sitting next to in the meeting room across the table from the project coordinator Kim Benjamin, a tall, slim forty-year-old, who had been on the project over a year at this point, some would say he "ruled with an iron fist."

"Well," said Tom, "I have talked it over with Kim before we met, hmm, we think it's the way forward." Before Sam could reply Kim said.

"The thing is Sam, we can't stop this as it is vitally important that we get the drainage system connected as soon as possible. The winter is here and should we get any of the massive storms that can arrive at any time here, well you can appreciate it could close the runway, possibly for days, which I can assure you I will not allow to happen."

"Kim, I totally understand all of that, and you know I always want us to work together, only," she chose her words carefully, "it's very dangerous, with unexploded gelignite laying in a trench with machines and rock breakers working all around it, we know what happened last time."

"That's why we need a watcher, he can be there all the time, looking out for jelly, and Kim has agreed to pay the person double time." Tom put in.

As she told Bob later she couldn't help saying, "that seems the answer all the time here, paying double time to get dangerous work done." There was silence for a few moments then broken by Kim who stood up and started to walk around the table, which was always an indicator he was about to end the meeting.

"Sam, as you know this site is like no other in the whole world, we have to do things, well, things we would not do another time. These men are here to earn as much tax-free money as possible, I will leave it to you and Tom to set up. But you both must understand, that work carries on at all cost, I do make myself clear, don't I?"

Before anyone could reply he continued, "good, I will look forward to hearing what you have set up. Sam, I know you are very capable of instructing the workforce how to carry this work out safely. Thank you for coming, good day." He rounded the table and left the meeting room with the two safety officers still in their chairs.

*

After Sam Crisp and Tom Smith left the drainage dig Bob looked at his watch and said to Ed as they got in the Land Rover, "do you know what Ed, it's ten past four, lets bunk off early."

"What before five thirty, you never do that?" Came the surprised reply.

"Well, do you know what Ed, once in a blue moon won't hurt, will it, I fancy having a hot shower for once, how about you?"

"You're the boss, Boss."

"That's it then, park around the back of the camp so that the Rover is out of the sight."

"No problem," came the reply from Bob's driver. It wasn't long after they left the drainage dig that they were walking down the corridor toward their respective rooms. They said their goodbyes as they entered their rooms next to each other.

"What the fuck are you doing?" Asked Bob as in took in the sight of one of Eastham's male cleaners a thick set man in his early fifties in blue overalls, who had the books and files which Bob kept all of the items and issues to bring up at the committee meetings with management, on the coffee table and was copying information into a notepad.

"What are you doing here? asked the cleaner.

"I live here, it's my room," Bob then banged on the adjoining wall between his and Ed's room and shouted, "Ed, get in here." It was only moments before his driver joined them, at which point the cleaner had picked up his belongings and was about to leave.

"You're meant to be at work?" The cleaner said.

"Don't worry why I am here. Ed, I want you to witness this, this fucking tosser," he pointed at the cleaner, "is copying my committee books, took them out of my wardrobe."

"I've got to go," said the cleaner as he made for the door which the two co-workers blocked.

"You are going nowhere until you give me your name and who told you to do this, and I want that paper work?" Demanded Bob as he pointed to the notepad in the cleaner's hand.

"I don't have to tell you anything, now let me out."

"LET YOU OUT! I'll fucking knock you out," Bob shouted as he held up his fist.

"Then you will be sacked and lose all your money." Responded the cleaner.

Before Bob could reply Ed held the committee man by his arm and said, "Bob let him go, don't get yourself in trouble, let him go."

"You haven't heard the last of this," said Bob as he pushed himself past the cleaner into his room, "get the fuck out of here you wanker!"

*

"That's well out of order," said Bill from his top bunk at the nightly meeting in his and Bob's room, with Bob sat on the side of his bottom bunk and Sam and Colin in the armchairs.

"I am so angry," Bob reported, "I can't believe it," he thought for a minute and said, "well I can really, nothing would surprise me here."

"When's your committee meeting? Asked Colin,

"Tomorrow afternoon, I feel like telling them to poke it."

There was a joint, "Nooo," from around the room.

"Bob," said Sam, "you are the one who is always telling people to stay calm and not to poke it, in some ways you could take it as a backhanded compliment."

"WHAT?" He asked.

"It's because you are doing a good job, if you were not they wouldn't be doing this, I bet."

"I think Sam is on to something there Bob," said a voice from above him, "why go to that trouble if they were on top of everything, no I think she's right, you have them rattled."

"Oh, I just don't know, it has just really cheesed me off so much." At that point the door opened to show Ed who said, "just to let you know I am off to play snooker, with my mate Joe, from home who has just come out."

"Is the snooker room open? Asked Bill.

"Yes," came the reply, "it opened last night, we have a table booked for eight, see you later." Ed disappeared.

"Right," said Colin as he got up, "I've got to go also, see you later." He also left the room.

"You're not going to like this Bob," came the voice from above, "but he is seeing Sally again, when we came back the month before you, I saw his wife seeing him off at the departures gate at Heathrow, kissing him, then when we got airside he met Sally at the bar and was kissing her!"

"Do you know what Bill, I have heard that," Bob got off his bunk and sat in the empty armchair next to his girlfriend who then held his hand, "I really don't give a monkeys toss what he does anymore, if he wants to throw his marriage down the drain, fine, let him, all he cares about is getting his leg over, I really don't care about him anymore!"

"Oh, come on," said Sam, as she squeezed his hand, "that's not you Bob English, you are a caring person, you once said to me you should never give up on anyone!"

"Well," came the reply, "with everything of late, you know, the divorce, people's problems here, the drugs, jelly in the trench, raping's, now this spying on me, I really don't like to say this, but I really feel stressed out."

"Oh Bob," Sam kissed him on the cheek, "I am going to help you unwind."

"Oh, by the way," said Bill, "I am still here before you two get up to anything!"

"Oh Bill Terry," Sam replied, "you need to sort your mind out, and stop reading those dirty mag's that you hide every time I turn up," she got up before anyone could reply, "have either of you two ever meditated before?"

"No," replied her boyfriend, "I have thought about it."

"That's for the drug smoking hippies, isn't it?" Asked Bill.

"Not at all," Sam said, as she pulled Bob out of the armchair by his right arm, "lay on your bunk with your arms at your side," she turned the small reading light on that was clipped to Bob's bunk, then walked to the door and turned the main room light off, "I am going to help you both relax."

"You meditate?" Asked Bob.

"Yes, I teach Yoga and meditation at home."

"Is there anything you don't do?" Smiled Bob.

Sam gave a small laugh and said, "I've never been shot out of a cannon, not yet anyway," she laughed, "right, now I am going to talk to you both, you are going to close your eyes, and imagine you are doing what I tell you, but do not fall to sleep. You need to breathe through your nose, down to your stomach, then gently blow it out, keep doing that, okay?" She got a joint, "okay."

She sat down in her armchair, "right, you are at the top of a large staircase, below to your right is a large hallway with nothing in it apart from a black and white tiled floor, and a door at the bottom of the stairs that is half open, and has the sun shining in. There are twenty steps down, and you are going to count them in your mind, backwards as we go down. Twenty, nineteen," she continued until they got to one then onto the floor. "Out of the door into the sunlight, and on to a gravel path, feel and hear the gravel below your feet, feel the sun warm on your face. To the right over on soft green cool grass is a fish pond, we are going to walk on the cool grass, then look at the fish," At this point snoring could be heard from Bill's bunk. "Ok," Sam continued in her soft tone, "look at the fish swimming." Sam then got up and tapped Bob on the shoulder, he opened his eyes with a shock, Sam put her fingers to her lips for him not to talk then by holding his hand pulled him off the bunk, and motioned towards the door with her head, they left the accommodation leaving the snoring Bill in the semi darkened room. "How do you feel?" She asked as they started to walk to her room.

"I feel amazing, it was like I was there, in fact at one point it was like I was looking down on myself."

"That means you were really in the zone; do you feel relaxed?"

"Yes, I do,"

"Good, now I don't want to hear any more about telling them to poke it, as you said to me we are down to our last few months, then we will be in Algeria, together, and Bob you are much bigger than that, we will do this together, help each other when times get hard."

They got to the door that lead outside and to the road they had to cross to get to the staff block and the female corridor, they walked to Sam's room hand in hand without saying anymore, when they got to her door they stopped and she said, "Mr English, would you like to come in for, oh let's say, a cup of tea and a biscuit, and possibly a kiss and a cuddle?"

"The latter sounds very intresting to me Miss Crisp."

*

"Well I think we should tell them to poke it," said Reg as he and Bob walked to the meeting room the next afternoon after Bob had told him what happened the day before.

"No Reg, then they win, no, we are here to support the lads, let's not let them tosser's spoil it!"

"You know I always back you Bob and we work well together," Bob nodded his agreement, "but there are times."

"I know," came the reply, "and it was my first thought, but I think we have done good for the lads at times here, and, well," Bob stopped to talk to Reg. "I don't want to give up on it." It was Reg's turn to nod his agreement, "so come on Reg lets go and give them what for, oh by the way, I am going to wait to the end to bring up what happened yesterday."

"That's fine," replied Reg as they entered the meeting room.

There was a full agenda for the meeting, the two committee men sat in their usual seats in the middle of the long table with the door behind them. Kim Benjamin was flanked on each side by Welshmen, both section managers, Arran Jones and Roger Clifford.

Some of the items to be discussed were, that hot food for lunch would start to be delivered each day to sections, they were like airplane meals, but could only do one section per day, so it worked out that it would be about two weeks in between each section having one, so a rota had to be drawn up.

There were issues about lads' hours, some complaining that they had not been paid the correct hours they had worked at David Antony section, he was now running the Tank Farm, also the lads complained how much he had been pushing them, Bob was asked to go and talk to him and the workers.

There had been a report about a worker being stabbed in the back the night before, Bob refrained from saying, "that's about right for this place," and instead agreed to see Karl about it. Mental health was brought up, as there had been a lot of problems of late with many workers doing some very odd things. Bob said most of the problem was men having to be there for six or seven months at a time, he was told, "it is, what it is!" But it was agreed that he and Reg would put the word about that the lads could see them about mental health issues if they did not want to see the Doctor.

There had been a dock strike in the UK would coincid with The Kenya that would be held up in Cape Town when it arrived there for urgent repairs, so it was possible they could maybe not get new supplies of food etc for two months and things could run out. It was agreed to tell the lads at the next workers committee meeting, that coming Sunday.

The blasting was brought up, and someone had been found as a watcher, Sam and Bob were going to make sure this was all in place correctly, Sam had written out how to approach the work in a safe manner that morning.

After some other items, Kim was about to draw the meeting to a close, when Bob said in a calm tone, "there is one more thing Kim."

"What is that Bob?" The committee chairman explained what had happened in his room the day before, Kim showed real surprise at the news, and asked the other two managers if they knew anything about this?

Arran said, "I do get information from foreman and managers from time to time, but I really don't know where they get it from."

"Who gives you the info? Asked Reg.

"Oh," came the reply, "it comes from many sources, it would be unfair to name anyone in particular, it's just information they pick up from time to time."

"Look gentlemen, I am not sure why this person should have done this, but if you leave it with us you can rest assured it will be looked into. With saying that, I think that closes the meeting, thank you."

Reg and Bob looked at each other then stood up, said their "goodbyes," and left the meeting room.

"Right," continued Kim, "who has been putting the cleaner up to this Arran?"

"It was George Connors getting the info, but since he has been gone the cleaner has been passing it on to David Antony."

"I did wonder how you knew so much all the time, have we been paying this chap?"

"I believe the lads get some petty cash and they give him a tray of beer every time he does it, which was just before our meetings, he has been doing it for months and months, unfortunately I think that will be the end of it now."

"Well," said the project coordinator as he stood up, "we shall have to find some other way of getting our information."

"The thing is Kim," replied Arran as he joined him on his feet, "there is his driver Ed, and I believe one of our safety officers is in fact having, hmm, shall we say, having a relationship with Bob English."

"I do hope it's Sam Crisp and not Tom Smith," laughed Kim, "I will leave it with you then Arran, good evening gentlemen."

*

Ed had not been feeling very well with an aching back and swollen foot, so Bob told him to have the morning off, "go to see Doctor Death and get yourself sorted." That meant Sam was driving the pair of them to the Tank Farm as she had little faith in Bob's driving skills. "I meant to mention," put in Bob as they started their nine-mile journey, "now we are, hmm, well, now we are." He appeared to have run out of words, Sam finished the sentence for him.

"Are you trying to say, now that we are lovers Mr English?" Asked Sam with a smile on her face as she glanced across at her passenger.

"Hmm, yes."

"Continue sir."

"Well, you never mentioned it, but, aha, are you on the pill?"

The driver smiled, "that would mess our future plans up, I mean a little Bob English turning up."

"I didn't mean that."

"I am kidding you Bob, and no I am not on the pill, and that is because I want your babies."

"WHAT?" His head snapped around towards the driver.

"Bob I am joking," she laughed, "I can't have babies."

"Oh."

"It's a very long story," she continued as they made towards April Ridge, "but I had a lot of problems as a child and was in and out of hospital for operations etc, and the upshot is, no I can't get pregnant, also I don't have to mess around with the pill, so that's a bonus out of it all," she laughed.

"Oh, I am so sorry, I didn't realise."

"Oh, I am well over it now, I hardly ever think of it these days. Are you ok with that?"

"I am fine, I've got my two girls, I wasn't thinking of any more, you've got to meet them yet."

"Yes, I've got to say I am looking forward to that. Oh, I forgot," she put her hand inside of her jacket pocket and pulled out some paper, "I looked up what your dream meant," she passed it across to him, he opened it and started to read out loud.

"Coughing represents your fear or dissatisfaction of the future. You need to put some distance between yourself or others. Coughing up blood represents wasted energy, you are spending too much time on counterproductive activities."

Bob thought for a short time then said, "wow, I think there is in fact a lot of truth in that, I am going to give that a lot of thought, can I keep it please."

"It's yours, to keep."

"Thanks, I wonder what it means to dream of shagging your best mates' wife, like Colin did of my wife Jane last year?"

"It means he's a horny sod," they both laughed at this comment as they proceeded towards the Tank Farm.

The wind was blowing off the sea and it had just started to rain as they approached the site close to the start of inlet to West Cove which was situated past the ship and the Lay Down Area where all the plant and containers were stored.

The site set up, offices, canteen, toilets and stores and a small concrete batching plant were at the entrance to the site to the left of road. The tank bases and surrounding aprons that were being built covered a very large area to the right of the road. As they turned into the parking area in front of the offices a front-loaded small dumper passed them full of concrete after just leaving the batching plant, headed for the one-metre high retaining wall shutter that had the concrete pour on going at the time.

They parked the Land Rover and decided to part company, Sam to inspect the safety aspects of the site and Bob to talk to the workforce, they put their white safety helmets on and headed off, agreeing to meet back at the office to talk to David in approximately thirty minutes.

Bob had talked to many of the workforce when he arrived at the batching plant to talk to the workers along with their charge-hand Butch Dickens a man in his early fifties from Newcastle upon Tyne in the north east of England. "Hi Butch, how are you?" Asked Bob as he held out his hand to greet the person who had become a friend over the last fourteen months or so.

"Oh, I am ok," he said as he removed the dust mask from his mouth, and dusted down his cement covered yellow overalls that were covered in the said dust, they shook hands and Bob said.

"Have you got a minute to chat?"

"Of course, Bonny Lad, always got a minute for you, but it will have to be just a minute, we have got two dumpers on the go here for that concrete pour," he pointed, "we are flat out."

"Well Butch that's what I want to talk to you about, we have had some of the lads on to us about, well, not getting paid all their hours and also how much they are getting pushed, by David Antony."

"Oh, he just does not leave us alone, I mean he is on our case all the time, push, push, push!"

"I heard you had a fight with Norman Jepson the concrete ganger?"

"That was meant to be between us, I could get sacked for that you know?"

"I know, but I will make sure that does not happen, what did happen Butch?"

"Oh, it was because of the pressure, the day was awful, I mean it was blowing a gale all day, pouring down, rain, snow, hailstones, you name it. The carpenters, steel fixers and the rest of the lads had been allowed to go. David said we had to stay and start a new concrete pour, I mean even with these things on," he looked at his yellow plastic overalls and said, "we were all soaked to the skin, it was so bad. Norman came down to me and said we needed to go faster. We had just stopped for a cup of tea in the afternoon, well what can I say, one moment we were shouting at each other, the next, well we were rolling on the floor, I don't know how it happened?" Butch thought for a moment and then said, "well I do, I pushed him over, he then got up and punched me in the mouth, David knows, but said he would not say anything."

"I bet he did, look Butch, thanks for that," he put his hand on his shoulder and said, "I am going to see David now."

"Bob," the charge-hand pleaded, "I really can't afford to lose this job, I mean I am paying off some really heavy debts, please?"

Bob shook his hand, "I will make sure you are ok." He turned and headed for the office and met Sam who was waiting outside. It was now pouring down with rain, and the wind was also a lot stronger."What do you think?" Bob asked the safety officer.

"The whole site is a real mess, it has really gone downhill since we were last here, which I don't think has been that long, I will look at my records when I get back to the office."

"It's since David has taken over, it seems the lads are falling out with each other as he is pushing them so hard. Come on Sam, let's go and see what he has got to say for himself." The pair went into the green port-a-cabin which held his office, he was behind his desk writing when the two entered.

"Come in, grab a chair, Bob, Sam. What can I do for you, I saw you arrive and thought you would come and let me know you were on site."

"Right, sorry, apologies for that David, " Sam replied. "We have had a walk around, and the truth is the whole site is a total mess, there are possible trips and falls all over the place, just waiting to happen."

"I know it's a bit untidy but we are very busy, I will get the lads to have a tidy up in the near future."

"No David, you will stop all work and get it sorted, NOW!"

"Well Sam, I know you mean well, but our program is so tight here, we have these large tankers on the way in the next couple of months, and the truth is, that is the main thing I really have to think of at the moment."

"David," Sam continued, "I am not asking you to get it done, I am telling you, if you want me to stop work here, I will."

"I think Kim would have something to say about that."

Sam took her time and said in a calm tone. "Look, I know what you are up against, and I know Kim wants you to get everything sorted on time, and I can go to him, but I don't want to do that. I am here to work with you, now if you stopped work for a few hours and get the lads on it, well it would make a massive difference, make the site a lot safer, and, well, I will not report it."

"Ok, I want to work with you, we have a concrete pour on at the moment, it will be over soon, I will get everyone on it then, is that okay?"

"We will be back later David." She promised.

"That's fine, we will be on it this afternoon."

"Thank you, David, I think Bob wants a word." David turned his attention to the committee chairman.

"YES, BOB?" He asked in an impatient tone.

"I have had some of your lads come to me, there seems to be a lot of bad feeling around here at the moment, most of it seems because you are pushing them so hard."

"At the cost of repeating MYSELF, we have got so much to do in such a short space of TIME!" He raised his voice to make this point.

"David," Bob put his hand up in front of him, then continued. "I do understand that, but the lads have been fighting and the morale seems to be very, very poor." The section manager went to speak but Bob stopped him. "Let me finish please, we have to sort this. Now I will help you anyway I can, but if these lads are working overtime they should be paid those extra hours, they need to have their correct breaks, and if they do work through their breaks, you need to pay them extra for that."

"Look Bob, I have a budget here, it's just like a site at home, I need." David was interrupted by an out of breath Paul, a concrete worker who rushed in, and said.

"Quick, there's been an accident, Norman our ganger has been crushed by a dumper, he's in a bad way." Everyone in the office jumped up and followed Paul a few hundred yards to where they found the laying gangerman with a crowd of workers around him. "He was stood in front of the dumper shovelling the concrete out of the bucket, I was driving, I am sorry but it was me, I knocked it into gear as I was getting off to help him and it jumped forward and crushed him between the dumper and the shutter."

Bob was the first on the radio and explained to the controller what had happened and told them he thought he would need to be airlifted to the army hospital in Stanley.

He was told there was nowhere for a helicopter to land at the Tank Farm, and instead of waiting for the ambulance to come down was it possible for Bob and Sam to bring him to the office compound and the helipad, which he agreed to.

Bob explained to David and Sam what they were going to do. The cushions from each side of the seating areas in the rear of their Land Rover were put on the vehicles floor and Norman was lifted onto them, an old blanket was found in the front of the Land Rover and put over the injured worker. While he was still conscious he seemed to be bleeding from many areas, and was crying out in pain. Bob rolled him onto his side into the recovery position, so that he did not choke on blood, liquids and possible vomit. The committee man stayed on his knees behind Norman so that he could hold him and stop him from rolling one way or the other.

Sam drove as fast as she could without causing the injured man too much pain, but as the permanent West Cove road had only recently started construction, most of the journey would be on the haul roads, which contained a large amount of pot holes, which the driver was trying to avoid, but they now seemed to be in the middle of a full-blown storm. With the windscreen wipers on full it was very poor visibility for the driver with rain bouncing off the glass screen in front of her.

Bob kept talking to Norman who seemed to be drifting in and out of consciousness, and at times he would even shake him and say things like, "Norman, don't go to sleep, stay awake Norman."

They were about one mile from the turn off to the office compound and the helipad when the controller came on the radio and said, "Bob, they can't get a helicopter up in this, it's too rough, depending where you are, it may be best to carry on the Stanley Road, they have sent an ambulance from Stanley, you should meet it at some point, is that okay?"

"That's fine Nick, we can do that, did you hear that?" Bob called out to his driver girlfriend.

"No problem," Sam said over her shoulder, "how is he?"

"I really don't know," came the reply, as Bob shook him again and continued to talk to the injured man. It seemed an age as they drove the forty miles in the storm towards the capital, they were in fact very close when Sam saw the blue flashing lights come into view, she stopped the Land Rover flashed the headlights, wound her window down and waved her arm for them to stop, which they did. Pulling up then manoeuvring behind them. Two army medics transferred Norman into the ambulance and disappeared into the storm.

The two possible life savers sat in the front of the parked Land Rover and were almost too exhausted to talk when Sam's radio came to life, it was her boss Tom Smith. Sam explained what had happened and where they were when Tom said. "Can you come back here straight away so we can go through what has happened and make the report out."

Sam picked some paper out of the glove compartment in front of Bob, and rustled it over the mouthpiece and said, "Tom you're breaking up, I really can't hear you."

Tom said very clearly, "Sam, can you," at this point she said.

"Tom," still rustling the paper, "I really can't hear," then she turned the radio off, she looked at Bob who had a very puzzled look on his face and said. "He can get knotted, if he thinks we are rushing back after what we have just been through, he's mad. We are driving into Stanley, and my boyfriend is buying me lunch at the Atlas, and we are both going to have a well-deserved beer."

Bob held her hand and said, "I'll drink to that Miss Crisp!"

Chapter 4

I Spy.

"Good morning Sam," said Arran Jones as he sat down facing the safety officer as she sat alone at the six-person table at six thirty-five am in the staff canteen before she started work at seven. "Can I join you?"

"Of course," she wiped her mouth with a napkin as she finished her scrambled eggs on toast and pushed the plate away, "how can I help you Arran?"

"I was just wondering how everything was going, you have had a lot on, I mean sorting issues and things, how's it with the jelly?"

"I am up there with Bob this morning to see that everything is going okay, with the watcher and all, well let's say, it's as safe as it can be under the circumstances."

"Well done. Do you know what?" He did not give Sam a chance to answer, "I think what you have done here, well it's been amazing. I mean a woman doing your job, in this industry is one thing, but, well, doing it here, and your ideas, I just take my hat off to you."

Sam took a drink of her black coffee, put the cup down and said, "what do you want Arran?"

"Sorry?"

"What do you want? You never talk to me, even at meetings, let alone come and make small talk at breakfast, so what do you want from me?"

"Oh," said a very surprised manager, "there was nothing really, I just, hmm, wanted to see how everything was going?"

"Everything is fine thank you," she wiped her mouth again then stood up, "I have to go."

"Well, there is one thing, aha, maybe," he replied in a lower voice, "if you could sit down, again please?" Sam sat again. "Hmm, the thing is, well, hmm, let's say."

"Arran, I have an awful lot on today, could you just spit it out please?

"We, hmm Kim, was wondering if it was, maybe possible." The safety officer interrupted him and said.

"Kim was just wondering if as you have lost your spy, the cleaner, could I take over?" She stood up, and continued, in a slightly louder voice, that caught the attention of others eating their food, "no I will not be spying on anyone, I am not here for that, so you had best find another person. Good morning Arran," she left the table and headed for the exit door leaving Arran sitting on his own with a red flushed face.

*

Ed returned to work that morning, Bob had arranged a meeting with Don Brown the section manager at eight o/clock, he had asked Bob if he could have a private word with him. As they were travelling to Don's section, Ed as he drove the vehicle was telling the other two about his visit to the doctor the previous day, with his aching back and swollen foot.

"He told me to take my wardrobe door off and lay on that, for my back, I said bugger off, I will be charged £100 for damage!"

"What did he say about your swollen foot?" Asked Sam from her middle seat.

"It's just a joke." Ed continued.

"What happened?" Put in Bob.

"Well after the wardrobe door, I told him about my foot, and he said, 'can you get your work boots on?' I said yes, I think so, and he said, 'good, you can go back to work then,' he didn't even bloody look at it!" This brought laughter from the other two.

"Well, do you know what happened to Jimmy the tyre fitter?" Asked Bob.

"What?" Asked Sam.

"His roommate went to the medic the other night and said Jimmy was having chest pains and was really unwell in his room, and the medic said, 'has he got pains in his legs?' His mate said 'I don't think so,' and the medic said, 'well tell him to walk over here then.' He had a heart attack, it's worked out he has had three in all, one the next morning walking to the medical centre, and is now in hospital in Stanley, they are flying his wife out as they don't think he is going to make it!"

"Bloody hell," came the joint reply. "The medic should be sacked for that," put in Ed.

"Well," continued Bob, "I don't want to see anyone sacked, but I will bring it up at our next meeting, and the medic should be brought to task over it."

"Totally agree," put in the safety officer. They continued their journey to Section 41, which was north west of the airfield. It was a large section which would have ten large storage units with offices within them and also a concrete frame office block at the start of the site for administration purposes. Bob was dropped off at the start of the site, where the site set up was. To reach the office he had to pass the joiners' workshop, which outside had an eight foot by four foot sheet of plywood, fixed to 6x3 inch wooden timbers concreted into large cut down oil drums, laying the eight foot way it was painted white with red painting on it, at the top it said, "Ship-Odometer," below that was a painting of The Kenya, and below that was a semicircle, at the left saying, Cape Town then one to fourteen, with West Cove at the bottom, then fifteen to twenty eight going from the bottom to the right, to Cape Town, again. There was a moveable arrow to point to the days. Bob looked at this on his way to Don's office with a pang of upset to see it was only just on its way back to the South African port.

After Bob had left his two co-workers for his meeting, Sam said, "I am going to have a look around the site Ed."

The driver replied, "can I have a word Sam, like, just between you and me?"

"Of course, Ed," she took her safety helmet off and turned to him, "what is it?"

"Oh, this is upsetting, I mean, hmm, not good."

"Ed, what is it?" She asked in a very concerned tone.

"I've been asked to spy on Bob, I mean, his info about what the lads are after and everything."

"By Arran Jones?"

"Yes, how do you know?"

"He approached me this morning, I told him where to get off, what did you say?"

"I, I said, well, hmm."

"You said you would."

"Oh, fucking hell, sorry Sam," she just smiled at the swearing, "I really like Bob, and he has done a lot for me, and has become a really good friend, but I really can't afford to lose this job, Uncle George always asked me to give him info, which I think Bob knew, but, well this was different, Arran made it sound very serious. What can I do Sam?"

"We are going to think about it, and work it out Ed."

"Should we tell him?"

"Nooo, I don't think so, well not at the moment anyway." Sam thought about this and said. "No, I would like to be honest with him, but depending which Bob English we told it to, there could be some very bad results."

"How do you mean?" Asked a puzzled looking driver.

"Well there's one Bob English who would take it okay and want to out think them, then there's another Bob English who would storm over to the offices and tell them to poke the job up their arse, and the way Bob has been of late, I mean mentally, well he's not in a good place at the moment. He has had so much happen in a short space of time. I think he would do the latter, and the truth is Ed, none of us want that, do we?"

"No, not at all," came the reply.

"Look Ed," she put her safety helmet back on, "let's not say a word, keep it just between us, let me think about it, he knows they have been spying on him, so let's take it from there."

"I could tell them lies, I mean make things up." Ed replied.

"Nooo, because they would get rid of you when they found out. No, let me think about it, and if Arran asks you what you have found out, say he has said nothing to you and he keeps his books close to himself at all times because of what happened with the cleaner, tell him he said he does not trust anyone here anymore."

"That's good, thanks Sam."

She got out of the Land Rover thinking to herself, "this is not going to be easy at all."

*

"Come in Bob, do you want a drink?" Asked Don the forty-two-year-old, five-foot-nine, slim build dark haired section manager from Portsmouth in Hampshire. Bob had walked through the office door which was in the end wall of the twelve by thirty-two-foot port-a-cabin. In front of him was a counter with a hatch and door in the right-hand side, almost like a shop, the office side of the counter was carpeted.

"Oh yes please, this is aha, fancy," commented the visitor, as he looked around the office from the counter and read a notice on the wall that said. "Do not enter beyond this point unless invited by the Section Manager, then shoes or boots must be removed."

"Come in, oh, can you take the boots off, hmm, please?"

Bob started to do as asked but did think the, "please," was an afterthought. The first thing Bob thought after his footwear had been removed was how cold the floor was, he then entered the office and sat on the chair in front of the desk at the far end of the windowless office. "Black or white coffee," asked the manager as he poured the liquid from its glass electric coffee maker on top of a fridge between a four-drawer metal filing cabinet and a six-draw drawing chest.

"Oh, white, no sugar please." Bob sat on the chair with his feet off the cold floor. As Don walked past him and put the coffee on the desk in front of him and his own on his side of the desk, he noticed Don had a very nice-looking pair of carpet slippers on. "Thanks Don, what is it I can do for you?" He asked as he sipped at the drink.

"Well, it was Karl Davis who said to have a word with you, I think you know about the machine smashing the office up, this is a new one, it's metal, let the tosser's try and smash this one. I haven't long had the carpet fitted."

"How did you get that?"

Don tapped the side of his nose and said, "it's not what you know in this life Bob, it's who you know."

"I think your right Don. Yes, Karl told me about the office and someone on the radio then the wheel nuts on your Land Rover."

"It went quite for a while, then the other day I got here in the morning, and taped to the office door was a note saying, 'You have not got long left.' The thing is Bob, they don't scare me, if someone wants to have a go, not a problem, let the fucker come and have a go, I don't do this hiding shit."

"I know they are now bringing in night passes, so anyone found on any sites after work hours has to have a pass, if they are on nights etc. And security is increasing night patrols. "

"Yes, Karl told me they are bringing that in, I just don't know why anyone would want to do this, I don't get it."

"Have you upset anyone?" Asked the committee man.

"Oh yes, of course, all the time, I don't take any shit Bob. I am here to get a job done, half of these tosser's would not be able to hold a job down at home. Look, at home there's three million unemployed, there are riots in the streets, most of this lot are lucky to be working at all. This is the construction industry Bob, you have been at it a long time, I don't need to tell you it's a hard game."

"I know Don, but the thing is, well you have to be a bit reasonable with the lads."

"Reasonable?" He raised his voice, "I look after these lads, they know the score, get the fucking work done, or their off, next ship, fuck off back to the UK," he pointed past Bob. "I've got Kim's backing, you know he won't take any shit." He seemed to calm down after he had his rant as he took a sip of his own coffee.

"It's different here Don, these lads are away from home a long time at a go, there's a lot who have struggled, mentally, it's just not like a job at home." The manager went to reply as the office door opened to show a middle-aged tall dark-haired worker.

"Don, we need you to." The worker was cut off by the manager, who said.

"Fred, I am in a meeting."

"It's just."

"Fred, I will not say this again, I am in a meeting, now, FUCK OFF!!" The worker left the office without saying another word. "Now where was I, before I was so rudely interrupted by that tosser?"

"You were saying how well you look after the lads," smiled Bob.

"Well, they're just a bunch of fucking wankers."

"Don, I am not going to beat about the bush, you look after yourself here, and what you have said to me and what I have just seen, you don't give a fuck about these lads," he stood up and at once felt how cold the floor was again, he walked to the end of the cabin and started to put his boots on, "I am going to have a word with the lads, I will come back to see you later."

As he said this the door opened to show the female safety officer. "Hello," she smiled, "are you two finished?"

"For the time being," said Bob."

"Hi Don," Sam continued as she held a note pad in her hand, "I have just had a walk around your site and there are a lot of items I want to show you."

"I haven't got time for this, I am very busy."

"It won't take long," she smiled, "can we have a walk around please?" Bob stayed in the office to see the outcome.

"Have you two just come over here to fucking wind me up? Your fucking boyfriend," he pointed at Bob, "was meant to come and support me, and the truth is, well he's as much use as a chocolate fucking tea cup, all he cares about is the fucking lads, he doesn't give a toss about me." Before either could answer he continued, "just fuck off," he pointed to the door, "go on, before I do something we will all regret." The two visitors looked at each other and left the office.

*

"Thank you for seeing us at short notice," said Sam as she and Bob sat in front of Kim's desk in his office.

"Well you made it sound very important on the radio Sam."

"And it is," put in Bob, "we have just been to see Don Brown, and for want for another way of putting it," he looked sideways at Sam, who gave him support with a smile and a nod of her head, "well Kim, the lads lost it, he is on the brink of being out of control!" There was a silence while this information was given time to sink in, the silence was broken by the project coordinator who said.

"How do you mean, please explain?"

"As I said, we have just been to see him, he got very upset, and it ended with him threatening us, that if we didn't leave he was going to do us."

"DON said that?"

"Well," put in Sam, "his exact words were, 'just F off before I do something that we will all regret,' which to be fair is pretty threatening Kim."

"Well, yes," Kim continued after thinking for a few moments, "but are you sure you did not take it out of context?"

The pair looked at each other then Bob continued, "I was in his office when a chap came in to ask a question, and, well, he shouted, possibly you could say screamed at him, and told him to F off."

"His whole site is in a mess, unsafe in many areas Kim," the safety officer put in, "and when I asked him to walk around with me, well, he refused."

"When we left his office, I went and had a chat with some of the lads and they all said, that he is like that all the time," said the committee man, "and he has been threatened, as you know and the office smashed up as well Kim. I feel it's only a matter of time before something really bad happens."

"We need that section completed, and he does do a good job, he does get the work done," the project coordinator replied.

"But at what cost?" Asked Sam. There was silence as the last comment was given time to sink in. The female safety officer then continued, "I believe he goes on leave soon, who is taking over from him then?"

"Well he was going air bridge, so we can get him back soon, and the truth is we don't really have anyone lined up as we were going to get one of the other managers to cover it, keep an eye on it." Kim replied.

"I don't think he is in a good place Kim," Bob said, "he is like a coiled spring ready to uncoil. He's a section manager, he should have more control than he has, of himself I mean."

"If we let him go when he was on leave, oh, I really don't like doing this to him," continued the project coordinator, "he has worked really hard."

"It's better than something really bad happening," put in Sam.

"I know, I know, but I have got no one to replace him."

"I know someone," said Bob, "he is working as a foreman at the moment, and I know he could step up."

"Please tell me more Bob?"

*

"I am not moaning about joining you two here for tea and biscuits," smiled Wolfie as he sat in the armchair next to Bob in Sam's room, who was sitting on her bed. "But this is all a bit undercover so to speak, why could we not talk in the canteen?"

"You will understand," replied Sam, "Bob will explain, over to you Mr English," she made an action with her hand as if to hand over a microphone, Bob in turn pretended to take it.

"Thank you, Miss Crisp. Whichever way this goes Wolfie this has to stay between the three of us, for the time being?"

"Of course, lad, you know me well enough now, kept secrets all over the world. Oh, any news on Norman Jepson, who had the accident?"

"Yes, they have looked after him well in Stanley. I don't know everything, I think his worst injury is a broken pelvis."

"Ouch," came the reply from the visitor.

"I was told he will be flown home as soon as he is fit enough for the flight."

"Good, I like Norman."

"Right Wolfie."

"Yes sir?"

"Do you know Don Brown, he is the section manager on 'Section 41'?

"I do know of him, not much, hey, is he not the one someone has been on about killing?"

"That's him," put in Sam.

"Well," continued Bob. "He is on leave this month, and should be going air bridge like most of the managers, but he may not be coming back."

"He's jacking? Well that's a surprise," replied the visitor.

"Well, aha, no," Bob looked at Sam who nodded to him, "he may be, hmm, well, I think, aha."

"Spit it out lad," put in Wolfie. The reply came from Sam who said.

"He maybe, let go."

"SACKED?" Asked a very surprised Wolfie.

"Well, yes," Bob continued.

"Bloody hell, I would never have thought that. I thought he was doing a good job down there?"

"There are so many problems," Sam put in, "how he is treating the man and safety issues."

"I did hear he is a bit of an arse," Wolfie took a sip of his tea then asked, "what has this to do with me?" Again, the pair looked at each other, then Sam said.

"Bob has put you forward as a replacement."

"Replacement, replacement what?"

"Section manager," said Bob.

"Section MANAGER?" Came the shocked reply, "I am not a manager lad."

"You could be," smiled Sam, "you're a foreman now, the lads like you and you get the work done."

"Oh, I don't know."

"Well you want to get on in life, don't you?" Asked Bob, he got a nodded reply from a seemingly shocked Wolfie, which was a rare event. "I, we, put you forward because we think it is something you are not only capable of, but would really enjoy, stepping up too."

"I, well."

"Look," put in Sam, "Bob has done a deal for you, money wise and also you would have another section manager helping you out, both of us would help you. I will help you sort out all of the safety issues, Bob has said he will come down and chat to the lads to start things off. What do you think, Wolfie?

"Oh, my good god, you have a lot of faith in me, you two, don't you?"

"We do," came the joint reply.

"I was going to say I have never managed before, but there again if my memory serves me right, there was a time when I was in Peru or was it Chile?"

Before he could continue Sam said. "Come on Wolfie, we know you can do it, and do you know what, if it does not work out, you have had a go, you have stepped in when needed, got some extra tax-free cash out of it."

Then Bob continued. "And how good would it look on your CV, section manager in the Falkland Islands?" Wolfie put his cup of tea on the coffee table and put his hand out for them both to shake and said.

"Lads, Sam and Bob, I would say it would look very good, and I think it was Chile"

*

"Hi, Ed," the surprised driver who was standing beside his Land Rover in the office compound car park smoking while he waited for Bob and Sam who were in meetings turned to see Arran Jones who had crept up behind him.

"Oh, you made me jump, hi Arran."

"Any news Ed?"

"Oh, I haven't seen many newspapers lately," smiled the driver.

"Don't get smart with me my lad, you know what I mean, and before you say any more let me remind you that you were given this," he pointed to the Land Rover, "cushy job to keep an eye on English." The expression on the drivers face changed as he said.

"Sorry Arran, it's very hard since he caught the cleaner, I heard him tell his roommate Bill that he doesn't trust anyone here now."

"Right," came the reply as the manager saw the safety officer appear from out of the main offices and walk towards them, "we need info Ed," he then turned and left the driver alone as Sam approached.

"What did he want, don't tell me, he wanted to know what information you have from Bob?"

"He did Sam, and he mentioned about me having this job basically to spy on Bob, I just can't lose this job Sam."

"Okay Ed, it's okay" she ran both her hands through her dark hair, "we will work something out, don't worry, you will not lose your job, I promise you that," she smiled, "we will sort it.

*

"Thank you for seeing me Kim."

"That's fine Sam, what can I do for you?" The two sat alone in the meeting room. After Sam had finished talking to Ed she returned to the offices and requested to see the project coordinator, which she was told she could do if she came back in one hour which she had done.

"Look we know, and more to the point Bob English knows that people have been spying on him."

"Well, that's one way of putting it, yes I do know that, I have never asked, or sanctioned it, but over all, it has got to be said it has, well, let's say, maybe helped at times. Some of our staff seemed to take it upon themselves to do this."

Sam thought about her next words for a few moments, then replied. "The thing is Kim, what has happened has happened, we can't change that, but Bob has sorted a lot of problems out here, as you well know."

"Yes, I agree with that Sam."

"He has had a lot of problems here and at home, he has been stressed out with everything," the coordinator nodded his agreement. "I am not telling you what to do, but can I ask that, let's say, the hounds are called off our driver, Ed, it has put him in a very difficult position and it has upset him greatly."

"I can," he stood up to signal the meeting was about to end, "I confirm that will be carried out Sam." They shook hands across the table.

"Thank you, Kim," she turned to leave the meeting room, when Kim said.

"Sam, people may not believe it but I do appreciate what he, and Reg have done. I know I may not show it, but, yes, I do appreciate what they have done. I don't have a problem you telling him that." The female thought for a few seconds then replied.

"It may be better coming from you Kim. Bye for now." She turned and left the project coordinator pondering.

*

"How's it going being section manager then Wolfie?" Asked Colin as the two along with Bob, Sam, Sally, Ed and Bill sat having their Sunday evening meal in the canteen. The eight-person table which was against the window wall had Wolfie and Bill facing each other next to the windows, then Colin facing

Sally, then Ed facing Sam with Bob next to her at the end of the table.

"Well lad," came the reply, "I have only really just taken over, It's well, Don was there and I was put in as a foreman, then he was told he would be going on the Uganda and not the air bridge as he thought, and was also told he would be on a new section when he got back, he then had a big row with Benjamin, then he went sick and goes next week on The Uganda from Stanley, so it has only been a few days lad, but it been okay, I am getting into it. Everyone is helping me, Bob, Sam, Arran Jones pops in to see if everything is okay, the lads have all been good, so I will say it's going well."

"It has got to be an improvement from that tosser," put in Ed, "he was awful, I talked to loads of his lads, and I mean, they hated him and I talked to him just once and, well, he was just so rude, I think tosser is a good name for him."

"I worked for a bloke like him in, where was it?" Wolfie asked himself as he put some steak pie in his mouth off his fork, "Oh yes it was when I was working on the new railway in Oz, yes he was not very nice at all, I think tosser would be a good name for him also Ed."

"Well," put in Bob, "he will be gone tomorrow, and if he does come back he will be on another section."

"Did you get the newspapers you ordered from the shop Bob?" asked Colin.

"I did for a change," Bob replied, "they have not been saving them for me of late, also Colin in the first post we have had for almost two weeks I got our local papers sent by my Mum."

"Oh great, I will look forward to seeing them."

"I got a load of Glasgow newspapers today," put in Sally.

"I would ask to lend them when you are finished," smiled Bob, "but I don't read foreign languages." This brought a laugh from everyone apart from Sam who gave him a dig in the ribs with her left elbow and said.

"That's not very nice Bob English."

"Ouch, that hurt Miss Crisp."

"That's just reminded me," put in Colin, "I was thinking the other day that if you two ever got married, and you joined the names Sam, as some people do, you would be an English-Crisp."

This brought a round of laughter from everyone at the table and the joke teller was about to continue when Ed said.

"A very drunk looking Don Brown has just staggered in." They all looked towards the canteens entrance to see him stagger past the security guard who was at the doorway and head towards them.

"Oh shit," said Bob, "we don't need this crap."

"It will be fine," said Sam as she put a comforting hand on his knee under the table. No more was said amongst the diners as they watched him make a 'B' line towards them. When the new comer got to the end of their table he pointed at them all and in a drunken shouting voice said.

"Look at you bunch of fucking wankers', all of you, got me the fucking sack." The packed canteen had now fallen silent as they listened to Dons rant.

"No," replied Bob, "I don't think that's the case?"

"Well read this, you fucking arsehole," he pulled a letter out the right-hand pocket of his zipped up blue water proof jacket and threw it on the dinner table, as this was happening the guard at the door started talking into his radio. "It says my fucking contract has been terminated, and because of you," he pointed at Bob, "and you," he pointed at Sam, "you fucking bitch." He unzipped his jacket, as Bob stood up.

"Ok Don that's it, just go now please?" Before Bob could do or say anymore Don head butted him in the face with such force that he fell to the floor, crashing into the table on the way down, this was then followed by a kick which hit the laying Bob high in his chest. Everyone at the table stood up, as this happened Don pulled a sheaf knife with a long blade out of its case on his belt that had been hidden by his jacket until that point.

"Come on you fucking wanker's, I'll take you all on." The first person to move towards him was Sam, as this happened the knife waving Don took a few steps backwards, as she stepped over Bob who was starting to get up, Don said, "don't think I won't do you cause you're a fucking woman."

"Sam, leave him," called out Wolfie.

"Don, I have to warn you," said the advancing safety officer, before she could finish the drunken man with the waving knife said.

"Warn me, fucking warn me, warn that you're a bitch of a fucking women, who," before he could finish, Sam kicked her right foot into his right hand that was holding the knife sendingit spinning from his hand, while he still had a look of shock on his face, she span on her left leg, leapt into the air and with the flat of her right foot hit him with full force high in the chest, sending him crashing into the table behind him, giving the occupants of the table just enough time to jump out of the way.

"Warn you that you are going to get a kicking, you wanker," shouted Bill from his end of the table. The security guard now with reinforcements of three more came running over with a straight jacket that were kept in all the canteens and bars for any such incidents. Immediately they went about putting it on a very dazed ex-section manager and led him out for a night in the new jailhouse. Bob had managed to get to his feet as Don was being taken away, Sam's main concern now was her boyfriend who had blood pouring from his nose, the canteen manager had already brought over the first aid box and gave out bandages to Bob who was now on a seat.

"Well," said Bill as they all gathered around Bob, "now Sam, if you had just given me a chance, that was just what I was about to do."

"Sorry Bill," Sam smiled, as she kissed him on the cheek, "I will leave it to you next time!"

Chapter 5

It's all in the mind.

"I heard this morning, The Kenya is being taken off in August, after that we will be in and out of here by plane." Reported Bob, who sat in his usual passenger seat next to the window with Sam in the middle and Ed in the Land Rover on their way to the drainage dig area which was now running close to the east-side of the main hanger, which was to have a blast that Monday morning after he had his nose broken by Don in the canteen. He now had two strips of white tape across the brake, he and Sam had spent the remainder of the previous evening in the medical centre, he also had two large black eyes.

"No," said Sam, "I wanted us to have two weeks on it, doing nothing."

"Well Miss Crisp, we will just have to do a cruise sometime."

"I thought your contract ended a month before Bob's, Sam?"

"Oh, it does," they both at once realised what they had let slip, it was Sam who recovered first. "Yes, Bob and I are thinking of having a holiday together."

"Oh, that will be nice, are you not coming back after that Sam?" Ed glanced sideways at them as he asked the question.

"Yes, of course, why do you ask that?"

"Well, they send you Air Bridge as a rule, so you wouldn't have been on the Kenya with us riffraff." He smiled.

"Oh yes, I was going to ask to stay an extra month then to go on the Kenya with Bob, before," she cut herself off before she said, "we go to Algeria."

"Before what?" Came the reply.

"Before another six months in this shithole," put in Bob.

"You are coming back as well Bob, aren't you?" Before he could reply Ed continued, "I hope you both come back, I am going to have to, in fact I think I am going to be here for the rest of my life to clear the debts that fucking, cheating, two timing, fucking bitch of an ex fucking wife left me with, oh sorry for all the swearing Sam."

"That's okay Ed, as you know I am used to it, just turn off up there please," pointing ahead said Sam, hoping to change the subject, "it's quicker that way, I would like to get there before the blast."

"No problem, I don't like to go on about her, but when I think about what she done, well, I just, oh, I won't say anymore, well, fucking bitch." Sam and Bob looked at each other.

They carried on the haul road which was the short cut to the hanger, it was not as wide as the other roads and had pull in points should two vehicles meet, it was for Land Rovers only, which was pointed out by a large sign before the start, but it did cut a lot off the journey as it cut across the green and yellow rolling peat hills. As they passed a lay-by they saw Del Parker sitting on his road scraper and appeared to be stroking something in his lap.

"Oh, that reminders me," said Bob, "I have got to see Del soon."

"I think you should go to the canteen first and get a bone for the dog," smiled the safety officer.

It was just over ten minutes before the large green tin cladded hanger came into sight. As they arrived the area had been cordoned off with red and white bunting tape, and the keep clear horn was sounding, a Land Rover with its four red flags flying, two front and two rear to show it was carrying explosives passed the newcomers as they pulled up near the compound set up, which now had workers walking towards, for their lunch break.

Ed stood beside the Land Rover smoking a cigarette as Bob and Sam made their way to the blast area, meeting Connor Allen the tall Somerset man in his mid-thirties who was the, 'jelly in the trench watcher!' "How's it going?" Asked Bob as the three stopped to talk.

"Not, not, augh bad," came the reply from the jelly watcher, with a noticeable twitch and shake of the head and stammer in his speech that Bob had never noticed before.

"Are you okay with doing this?" Asked Sam, "it's a very dangerous job Connor."

"For, for, a, augh," his head shook more, "double tax-free time," he twitched and shook, "I'd walk, augh, on burning, coals."

"Oh, my good God," said Sam, "please don't do it if it is doing this to you."

"Only kidding you on," smiled Connor, "everything is fine, I am going to lunch," he laughed as he walked off.

"Wanker," said Bob to his back. "I will have words with him later," he continued in a not very happy tone.

"Oh, come on Bob, you have got to admit, he had us going?"

"Well, suppose so, still a bloody tosser." He mumbled.

"Here's Kevin the charge setter," pointed Sam to a small overweight man in his early fifties from County Durham who was laying out the cable from a reel to connect to the box which had a red plunger handle that was sat on the ground in front of them, as he made his way towards them.

"I thought he had been taken off the blasting, because of his drinking," Bob said to Sam before the red-faced man was in ear shot.

"Don't know," came the reply, "that's what I thought."

"I'll have a word," Bob continued as Kevin Henry walked over towards them.

"Hi Bob, Sam," he nodded his greetings.

"Are you okay Kevin?" The committee man asked.

"Yeah," came the reply as he stooped and started to wire up the box on the ground, "why, shouldn't I be?"

"We, aha, we thought you were off the blasting," answered Sam.

"Well, yes I was, but the two other lads have gone sick, so they have brought me back on to it." He answered as he stood up ready to turn the handle that would ignite the charge.

"I was told," Bob carried on, "you had been taken off it because of, your, hmm."

"You can say it Bob, because of my drinking, I am fine, Dr Death has got me on a course of injections to stop me drinking."

"How's that going then?" Sam asked.

"Oh great," he smiled, "I haven't had a skin full since," he thought for a second, then smiled again, then said, "since last night." Bob and Sam looked at each other as Kevin turned towards the blast area and turned the handle on the box.

What happened next, could only be described as a blast so big that the ground trembled beneath their feet and the whole area in which they were standing was within seconds covered in dust with bits of flying rock landing very close to where they were standing, they all including Ed ran away as the large dust cloud started to engulf them. They and other workers ran beyond the site compound before they felt it was safe to stop.

It was not long before Arran Jones came on the radio and said, "anyone near the hanger, what the fuck was that?" Another voice came on and said.

"The fucking hanger has just been blown up Arran, one side of it looks as if it has just been blasted with a giant shotgun, all one side is totally papered by rocks from the blast, it's a real mess, someone really OD on the jelly!"

"Oh shit," said Kevin to Bob and Sam, "I am off for another injection!"

*

"Thirty thousand pounds, you have got to be joking?" Said Wolfie as he sat in his new office behind his desk on 'Section 41' drinking tea with Sam and Bob.

"That's what they are saying it will be the cost to replace all the damaged cladding on the hanger, and of course it has been handed over now as well, even if there is work still going on around there, and I have been told there is no extra cladding on the island so it has to be ordered, made then brought over from the UK." Bob told the newly appointed section manager.

"Bloody hell, and what happened to Kevin the blaster?" Asked Wolfie.

"Oh, he's gone sick," put in Sam, "now there is none of the blasters working."

"I am going to see Kevin later today to see how he is getting on," Bob continued, "talking of which, how is our new section manager getting on Wolfie? The site is looking a lot better all ready."

"Only stand in manger lad, nothing official, yet"

"Well," said the safety officer, "we have had a good walk around and you have sorted out the list of safety items I gave you, thank you and well done for that."

"Well, I tell you lass, I don't get it with some of these managers, you look after your lads and nine times out of ten they will look after you."

"How are you getting on with them?" Asked Bob.

"Oh, it's good lad, I already knew a fair few of the lads, but between us," he started to whisper and motioned the two at the other side of the desk to come in closer with his hands, "we have got a couple of real odd ones here."

"There's odd ones all over this project," laughed Bob as he leant back in his chair.

"No, really, I have got one lad who has got a cage in his room with a cardboard cut-out of a mouse in it, he left a note for the cleaners to clean the cage out, and another who thinks he is Kentucky fried chicken."Both of the visitors laughed at this comment.

"The problem is," said Bob, "that there's a lot of them just after a medivac but of course people who put it on are going to make it harder for those who are mentally ill and are suffering."

"You're right Bob," put in the safety officer.

"So, what happened with Kentucky?" Asked the committee chairman.

"Well I really hadn't been here five minutes, I was walking around getting used to the site and all and this chap came up to me and said, 'can I go and see the doctor?' I said what's wrong? He said 'I think I am a chicken.' I am thinking this is a wind up, try it out on the new boy, I said ok, what's your name lad? He said 'Ken,' and I fell into it, hook, line and stinker by saying Ken what? And he said," the two guests said together.

"Kentucky," they all laughed.

"You're right," said the new section manager. "I said, ok lad, that's really funny, now what is your name? He said, 'Kentucky, and to prove I am not kidding, I will let you have eggs at half price.'"

"Oh, my good god," said Sam as they both laughed again, "what did you say?"

"Well the thing is he said it without a smile on his face, I thought, I can't be doing with this, so I said go and see Doctor Death then, when he was gone I radioed Arran and asked him to transfer him to another section if the doc does not sign him off, he's on the Tank Farm now"

"What about the chap with the cardboard mouse in a cage?" Asked Sam.

"Oh, he's okay," came the reply, "he only wanted an extra doggie bag to feed the mouse, I gave him one of them okay!"

*

"Bob, Sam, come and watch this," the pair had just finished work and were walking past the post office, it was getting dark and was feeling cold with the wind from the south and sleet in the air. A large post bag of mail with a very large sign on it saying, 'Mr K Harding' was by the post office door, near the flagpole that flew the Union Jack each day. The pair had been called over by Tony Linett a fifty-three-year-old, tall, well built, dark haired bricklayer from Slough in Berkshire.

"What is it?" Bob asked the laughing bricklayer.

"You know Keith Harding?"

"Yeah."

"Well, he has been moaning like mad that he does not get any post, says it is sending him around the bend, so I got ten of the lads together and for the past few weeks and we have all been sending off to these free post things in the newspapers and magazines. There are free samples, love letters, lonely hearts, all sorts in his name and Jim the post guy has been saving them up for us as they have come in, there is nearly a sack full now, so he is going to be given them tonight."

"That's rotten," said Sam.

"Yeah, but funny," smiled the mischievous Tony, "watch out here he comes." The three watched as the greying middle-aged Cornishman walked around the corner of the recreation centre and was about to walk past the post office to the accommodation block when Jim who was standing outside of the post office called him over.

"Keith, you've got post."

Keith stopped on the path under the now bright flood light and said, "what?"

"You've got post," Jim pointed to the bag, "it's yours, all yours."

"What? I don't get post, you know that."

"It's yours," Tony said as he walked over to the surprised newcomer, there was now a crowd of workers coming to see what was happening. Keith walked over to the post master who pointed to the sack with his name on. Keith opened the ties on the top of the sack and pulled out the first envelope with his name on it and read out loud the front, which said.

"Lose weight fast with, Plan C," he threw that to the ground then read the next. "Lonely? Don't be." This brought a roar of laughter from his co-workers, as he threw that to the ground and read the next one he pulled out. "Make your hair shine after just one wash." He went to throw that on the ground when Sam ran over and said with her hand out.

"Oh Keith, I'll have that if you don't want it, thank you very much," she said as she took it out of his hand before he could reply. Keith then picked the sack up and tipped the contents on the ground to a great roar from the gathered crowd.

"Now don't be saying you don't get any post," laughed Tony.

"Did you do this, you tosser Linett?" As he pointed at Tony.

"Well, maybe with a little help, come on mate, it was only a joke, I'll buy you a beer, he put his arm around the Cornishman's shoulder as they walked off towards the bar.

"Well Sam, for someone who thought it was a rotten idea, you got some shampoo out of it," Bob pointed at her hand.

"I still do think it was rotten to do that to him, not nice at all and it's in very poor taste to do that to a person who's is obviously very upset with the lack of mail. But guess what Mr English?" She smiled.

"What?"

"Let's have a look at what other freebies we can get," she fell to her knees next to the pile of packages.

*

"Drop me off up here, please Ed," Bob pointed to the end of the pioneer camp as the three approached the last cabin, the Land Rover pulled over. "I will wait here when I am finished with Del Parker from West Cove County Council," he smiled, "and John Trippier for you to come back from the Tank Farm, have fun with David Antony won't you Sam," he smiled to the safety officer, who kissed him once on the lips and said.

"Go on bugger off!" She punched his arm lightly.

Bob departed the Land Rover and walked around the last cabin and saw John Trippier, the short slim late twenties welfare officer with black shoulder length hair from Liverpool waiting for him. "Morning John."

"Hi Bob, Del is waiting in his cabin, I met him for the first time yesterday, he's a real odd one that lad."

"I think that's a fair assessment John. Did you meet his dog, Dodger?"

"No, what dog?"

"Don't worry, what's his problem this time?"

"Everyone got moved from here yesterday up to the camp, we need to clear this area for the new roads which run through the middle of it."

"Yes, I know that, what's the problem?"

"He refuses to go."

"Why?" Asked the committee man.

"Bob, I am not even sure where to start."

"Come on, let's go and get it from him." They walked towards one of the middle row cabins. Cranes and lorries had started to remove the camp that morning along with all the contents. When they arrived at Del's cabin it had been emptied apart from one bed, wardrobe and three wooden fold up chairs, one beside Del's bed with items on it including a radio alarm clock and two for sitting, which the two newcomers duly sat on facing Del who was sat on the side of his bed. There were dog bowls of food and water at the end of the bed, after the niceties he got up and handed some paper to each of them and said.

"I am not moving out of this cabin, you will see that on the papers," he pointed, "when I was on leave last time I went to Citizen Advice there's a copy of Squatters Rights and John you have a copy of the Human Rights Act, I have more so you can take them with you."

"Del," Bob looked up, "why do you not want to move up to the camp, it's got everything up there now?"

"First of all, Bob, there's a load of wanker's up there, I've heard all the stories you know."

"There's a load of them everywhere here," smiled Bob.

"The main thing is, that camp is going to get blown up very soon."

There came a joint, "WHAT?" From the two visitors.

"The Argies, they are only regrouping you know, once they have done that they will come and blow the fuck out of anything anywhere near that airfield."

"That's not going to happen Del, we are well protected here, by the RAF etc." Put in John.

"Mark my words son, it's going to happen," Bob went to speak but did not get the chance as Del continued. "I have hidden canned food in places away from here, Dodger and I," he patted a space near the bowls as he sat on the bed again, "will be able to survive for some time, I have been out on reconnaissance, I am trying to get some guns so when you are all captured I can come and pick them off!"

Bob stood up in alarm and put his hand out in front of him and in a very serious voice said, "no guns Del," he took a deep breath, "look Del, I am going to see Kim Benjamin to try and sort things out for you, but you must promise me you will not get hold of any guns?"

"It will be too late when they land here Bob lad."

"Promises DEL," he raised his voice.

"Okay Bob, only cause it's you asking."

"Leave it with me Del, I will sort it, but no guns Del!" The two left the cabin.

*

"Hi Sam, come in and sit down," David Antony invited the safety officer in, who had just inspected his site at the Tank Farm from behind his desk. "I have made tea." He pointed to a cup at the front of his desk.

"Thank you, David," came the reply as she sat down, with her notepad in hand and took off her safety helmet and placed it on the floor beside her.

"No Bob?"

"No, he is at another meeting, we are picking him up on the way back."

"I did think you two were joined at the hip, you are never far from each other, are you?"

"It's our job's David, you know that."

"Well I heard you two are going out with each other?"

"We knocked about together, now about the site." Sam continued wanting to change the subject as she was feeling uncomfortable with the questions. "It is looking a lot better, a lot tidier and safer, well done, I do have a few more bits here," she ripped a page off the pad and put it on the desk as she picked her drink up and took a sip, "but not much."

"He is only classed as a charge-hand you know?"

"Sorry?" Came the surprised reply.

"Bob, he's not a manager like you and me, I don't think he will ever make much of his life," he got up and started to walk around the desk, Sam put the cup down and got up.

"Right, I have got to go," she picked up her belongings.

"If you are just knocking around with him, how about us going out one night, having a drink, or" he smiled, "something?"

"Right, I have tried to be polite David, YES, I am going out with Bob and that's the end of it, RIGHT!"

"Sam, I heard what you did to Don Brown, your rock hard, I find it a real turn on" he smiled, "what do I have to do to replace Bob English?"

"David, I will continue to be polite, it's a two-word answer," she smiled, "and the second one is off!" She turned and left the office.

*

Bob sat in the meeting room with Kim, John and Joe Benson. The two who had been at the meeting with Del had explained everything that had been said to the others. The project coordinator said, "Well men, we need to remove him, that work cannot stop, it's very important, remove him by force if needs be."

"Right Kim, John and I have discussed it, and the truth is he is not in his right mind."

"Okay," said Joe, "why don't we medivac him."

"Look gentlemen," Bob continued, "he came out here on the first ship, he has been ganger on the haul roads right from the start, he has kept those roads open, come what may. I've seen him and talked to his lads, while he is, hmm, very strange at times.

But not to put too fine a point on it, he and his gang has kept the job going, he works bloody hard."

"That's all very well," said Kim, "but we can't stop the job, for someone who's."

"Not the full ticket," put in Joe.

"I think Bob and I have worked out what to do," added John. "We have talked to the manager on the road works down there and he said if he was in the far end cabin, we could leave that one and the shower block next to it."

"The lads working on the road will still need toilets, so they can use them, instead of going to the ship," said Bob.

"They could work around them," John continued. "The new road does not reach as far across as where Del's cabin would be."

Then Bob said, "the haul roads are nearly all up together now, his second contract ends in two months, don't offer him a new one unless he agrees to move up to the camp, as soon as he goes home move the cabin. Also, we think the doc should assess his mental health before he comes back here." There was silence in the room for a few moments, then it was broken by Kim when he stood up and said.

"Ok, that's it then, it's all sorted. I will leave it to you to organize it Bob."

The other three all stood and then Joe asked, "no one really thinks the Argentines will come back again, do they?"

After a short silence again Bob smiled and said, "well if they do Joe, I am off down to West Cove with Del and Dodger, he's got it all sorted!"

Chapter 6

Want a bet then?

"No, we said up front, no covering the kitty," snapped Bernie, a forty-five-year stocky built, bald headed ground worker from Sunderland in the north east of England. Covering the kitty is a term in gambling and in this case, Three Card Brag, when someone had run out of money, they could cover the cash with their cards and put it all to one side and the other players would continue with a new pot. This pot had grown to a sizable amount.

"Why not?" Asked the medium build and height, dark haired unshaven early thirty-year-old Glaswegian, Tim, who had a scar down the full length of the right side of his face. He was sitting at a small round table in the smaller bar late on a Thursday night. Tim had asked Bernie and two others if he could join their card school about an hour before, he had been losing heavily to that point.

"It's the rules we play with," put in Graham, a tall mid-thirties carpenter from Berkshire, "Bernie told you when you sat down, no covering the kitty, no seeing a blind man." Seeing is when two players are left in a hand and one pays the going rate at the time to see the others' cards, the highest hand wins. A blind man is when a player has not looked at their cards, he only pays half the going rate until he looks at his cards.

"So," continued Bernie, "we give a person ten minutes to come up with cash, no IOU's, cash or you throw your hand in."

"I've got cash in my room," Tim got up with his cards.

"No," said Carl, the twenty-eight-year-old short fair-haired drain layer from Rugby, "the cards stay here," he pointed at him, "you've got ten minutes."

Tim thought about what was happening with the people he did not know, and the amount of money which was on the table. He lit a cigarette from his pack on the table, placed his cards on top of his half full plastic pint glass then stood the burning cigarette from the filter end on the cards, then said, "if the ash is not on there when I get back, I have a blade, and I know how to use it."

He turned and left the bar. There was silence from the remaining card players for few moments, when Bernie said,

"Who invited that fucking lunatic to play?"

"I think you'll find it was your good self," answered Carl in a sharp voice.

"I did NOT," came the snapped reply.

"I think we all agreed," said Graham as he took his drink off the table.

"For fuck sake," shouted Bernie as he pulled himself away from the table, "don't touch the table."

"Fuck him," came the reply from Graham, "I've shit bigger things than him down the bog!"

"I'm going to see if I can have a look at what his bottom card is?" Said Carl as he moved near the empty seat next to him and bent his neck to look under the three cards.

"Fuck off, are you mad?" Asked Bernie, "just keep away from the fucking table."

"He won't do anything," replied Carl, as he went to bend his head again.

"This is no joke," came back Bernie, "we don't know this bloke, this place is totally full of nutters, you know that."

"Yeah, Bernie is right," put in Graham, "we don't want to get in any trouble, and end up losing our jobs because of this idiot."

"Okay, that's fine," reported Carl, as he looked at his watch, "but if he is not back in seven minutes I am taking his cards off the glass and he is out." Hardly a word was spoken among the three gamblers as they sat and watched the ash grow on the smoking object on top of the cards.

Carl announced, "there is one minute forty-five seconds to go," just before the fourth gambler returned with a handful of cash.

"Thanks for that time lads," said Tim as he sat down as if nothing had happened, he then took the cigarette off his cards and looked at them once more before putting his money in the kitty.

The game continued in almost silence until there was only Bernie and Tim left, Bernie just wanted to finish the game and get away from the bar and while he had a strong hand, ace, king, queen on the bounce (bounce in this case means three cards of the same suite) Bernie's were hearts, he said to Tim,"I will see you," as he paid his money to do so.

Tim laid his cards out and said, "seven, eight, nine on the bounce," (all clubs) he smiled.

Bernie laid his out and said, "A, K, Q on the bounce," he stood up and pulled the kitty to him and said, "right lads, I' am off."

"What?" Tim stood up across the table from Bernie, "you have taken a lot of money off me, you have got to give me a chance to win it back."

"It's late," Bernie replied as he started collecting his cash, "we can meet up another night."

"Where I come from a man gets the chance to win his money back, but there again, as a rule I play with real men."

"Where I come from," said Graham as he stood up, "people don't get threatened with a fucking knife when someone runs out of cash, JOCK!"

"You're a bunch of fucking wankers'," shouted Tim as he grabbed the table and tipped it over sending glass's and money spilling everywhere. As if in one movement the table tipper pulled a handle out of his green jacket pocket with his right hand, and with the fingers of his left hand exposed a five-inch blade of a lock knife.

*

"How much further before we turn back?" Asked Bob as he bent over breathing very heavily on the side of the haul road as Sam stopped a few metres in front of him jogging on the spot and asked.

"Are you okay?" She jogged back to her new running partner.

"No, I am knackered, as I said before," he straightened up, "as I said before, I can't remember the last time I ran, and this is before breakfast." It was a chilled morning, dawn had not long broken over the brown and green hillside they were running through.

"You said you wanted to get fit again," came the reply as she continued to jog on the spot, as if she had come a very little distance, "as a rule I turn around after about another mile, it will do you good. And also, it is best to run before you eat, come on, it will do you the world of good!"

"Oh," came the reply as Bob blew his cheeks out. As this was happening a Land Rover pulled up behind them and Ed jumped out.

"Good morning Ed, what brings you here?" Asked the safety officer.

"Morning Sam, Bob, I was just going to breakfast when Arran Jones found me and said I have to pick you both up for an urgent meeting, in the conference room as soon as I can get you there. I knew you were going to run this morning."

"They can get stuffed," put in Bob, "I'm going to get something to eat first." They all climbed in the Land Rover and Sam said.

"That was handy, Ed turning up when you were about to die Bob!" She smiled.

"I didn't put him up to it," said her red-faced running partner. As they drove away they could see a helicopter coming into land at the helipad near the camp.

*

Bob insisted they go to the canteen first, they then made their way to office compound armed with bacon rolls and cups of tea, they had been told in the canteen by one of the chefs, that was the last day of bacon for a while as they had run out and a lot of other things had nearly come to an end also.

Everyone was waiting for Sam and Bob at the large table, Kim, Karl, Arran and Reg who were all drinking fresh coffee. After the good mornings Kim said.

"There was a stabbing in the bar last night," this was greeted with gasps from Bob, Sam and Reg. "The chap is not too bad, but it was in the stomach, not too deep, the medical staff looked after him but we have had him flown to the capital this morning as a precaution."

"Who got stabbed?" Asked Reg.

"Graham Bentley," put in Karl as he looked at a file in front of him.

"I know Graham, a carpenter, he is working on one of the admin blocks," put in Bob.

"It seems they were playing cards when someone joined them and it ended in a fight," said Arran.

"We have seen some of those card schools, haven't we Bob?" Asked Sam.

"Yes, there are some really heavy-duty ones, some really large amounts of cash changing hands." replied her boyfriend.

"Two things here," continued Kim, "I want the chap who committed this offence caught and locked up ASAP, and I want to stamp out gambling here once and for all."

"I can't ever see that happening Kim," replied Reg.

"I wager it WILL!" Came the snapped reply.

"I'll have a tenner on that," smiled Bob. Everyone laughed at this apart from the project coordinator, who continued.

"I am not joking gentlemen and lady," he nodded to Sam, "gambling does nothing but great harm to people, and last night has proved it. Now what are we going to do about the perpetrator of last night's crime, Karl?"

"We know he said his name was Tim and he is Scottish."

"Is he with Eastham's?" Asked Bob.

"I don't think so, it was my first thought but they only have two Tim's and we have ruled them out already as they were both working. There were two others playing cards and they are going to look at the photos, believe it or not we have another fourteen Tim's here if that's his real name."

"How did it happen?" Asked Sam.

"Well," continued Karl, "there was a row over the cards, Tim tipped the card table over and went for one of the lads," he looked at paperwork in front of him, "Bernie, Graham tried to stop him and got stabbed for his troubles. Tim then ran away"

"That makes him the five T's," put in Bob.

"What?" Asked Karl.

Bob counted on his fingers. "Terrible, Tim, the table, tipper!" Again, this brought smiles from everyone apart from Kim who stood up and said.

"RIGHT, I want news that this person has been caught, soon, and I want this taken very seriously!" He left the room without another word.

Reg turned to his fellow committeeman and said, "I don't think he thinks much of your jokes Bob."

*

Bob and Sam went with Karl to see how the checking of the photographs was proceeding. Bob Smith from security was in Karl's small office going through the ID photos with Bernie and Carl when they arrived, the committee man and safety officer waited in the corridor as it was agreed there was not enough room for five people in the head of security's office.

When Bob Smith told Karl that they had "no joy" it was agreed that Bernie with Sam and Bob Smith and Bob with Karl and Carl would go around every section and talk to the managers and foreman to see if they could track Tim down.

They all left the office complex together and were walking to their respective Land Rovers when Bernie shouted, "that's him, that's him," he pointed, to a man walking across the car park towards them. Tim held his arms in the air as if to surrender and said.

"I have come to hand myself in, I only came on the last ship, can I talk to Bob English and Karl from security please. The two identified themselves by raising their hands, then Karl asked.

"What is it?"

"Can we talk, in private?" Came the reply. Karl looked at Bob who nodded, then the security manager said.

"Come to my office."

*

"If this, what? Well he is a villain, there is no other way to put it," Kim shook his head in disbelief at the news that he had been given him by Karl and Bob in the meeting room. "If he thinks, I, we, the company will guarantee the job of someone who uses a knife like he did, for information, well I am here to tell you gentlemen he is asking the wrong person." The silence in the room for a short while could be cut with a blade of a five-inch-long lock knife, until Karl said.

"Kim, Bob and I discussed this before we came to see you and, well, we knew you would not succumb to the demands of this, person." He pulsed for a moment before continuing, "this is what he asked us, to ask you and that is he knows where and when a fist fight has been organised, where a very large amount of money will exchange hands in bets and prize money. And that is what we have done."

"Kim," Bob put in, "we're not saying in any way we want this chap to stay, but you told us you want to stamp out betting, and the fact is if we bust this fight up and sack a few and give the rest final written warnings, well that would send out a very strong message to the rest of the workforce."

"And," continued Karl, "we then put up notices basically saying that gambling will not be tolerated, I think that will make people do a lot of thinking before they get involved." Again, there was a silence that could be cut with the same lock knife until Kim stood up and said.

"Gentlemen, I want this person, who you said is locked in our jail," they both nodded, "removed from here to the capital and charged with the knife crime. I then expect you both to find out where the fight is going to take place and jump all over it. Good day gents." He rounded the large meeting room table leaving Karl and Bob looking at each other for fresh ideas. After a short while Karl said.

"I may have it Bob, I can get up to five hundred pounds a year, to use in a way, let's say to make things happen, I haven't used any up until now. I think now is the time."

"What are you thinking?" Asked the committee man.

" Come on," Karl stood up, "I will tell you on the way to the police station.

*

Bob and Karl sat at one side of the desk with Tim at the other side in the small interview room in the project's police station. "I am not going to get my job back then?"

"No," replied Karl, "you are going to be charged and sent to the court in the capital, then sent back to the UK."

"That's it then," came the reply.

"I would still like to think you could give us the info on the fight Tim?" Asked the head of security.
"No way, I'm no snitcher."
"Well, you were going to before," put in Bob.
"That's when I was going to get something out of it, get my job back."
"You still can get something out of it," said Karl.
"How do you mean?"
"I will pay you," the security manager continued, "that way you can have some cash to go home with." Tim sat thinking about this then said.
"Two things, how much and I don't trust you, you're an ex-copper."
"Well the second first, you have no choice but to trust me, I give my word, I will make sure you stay here until we break up the fight, and I will give you the money before you leave. How much, I will give you two hundred pounds, its cash, for when you get home."
"Four hundred," came the reply.
"Two fifty."
"It's three fifty or there is no deal, I go home with all the info." Karl looked sideways at Bob then stood up and held his hand out and said.
" It's a deal."

*

"The thing is, that's why I am here." Said Bill as he laid on his top bunk smoking that evening, with Bob and Sam in the armchairs in the first two's room, after Bob had explained what had happened regarding the gambling.
"How do you mean?" Asked Sam.
"Gambling," he jumped down and sat on Bob's bunk with a letter in his hand, "I got in loads of debt, gambling."
"You never said," put in Bob.
"Ashamed I suppose, you two are the only ones who know here, you won't tell anyone, will you?"
There came a joint, "Nooo!"
"What did you bet on?" Asked his roommate.

"Oh anything," horses, cards, sport, two dogs pissing up a wall, anything, you name it. We nearly lost the house over it, the wife made me go to Gamblers Anonymous, or she was going to leave me."

"I'm sorry," said Sam.

"No, I was a real twat, I know that now, I haven't had a bet for over two years."

"Well done," put in Bob.

"The problem is now," he held the letter up, "I've just got this from the wife. One of the blokes I was into for money has moved in across the road from us, and he has said things to the wife, she is really worried.

"What's he saying?" Asked Sam.

"He has said about me being away, and last week he said he would have been okay if I had let the wife pay the debt off for me, in kind!"

"Oh, my good God," said Sam.

"Tell her to contact the police Bill," said his roommate.

"I want to pay some mates to give him a battering!"

"That's not going to help," said Sam.

"I know, but it's how I feel at the moment." The door to the room opened and Colin came in and asked.

"Bob, can we, hmm, have a chat please?"

Bob looked surprised but said, "of course, come in."

"Hmm, can we go, in, hmm, my room next door," he pointed left, "Ed's out playing snooker."

"Yes, of course we can," he got up and left the room with his friend. After chatting for fifteen minutes Bob returned to his room and Colin went out for the evening. Bob sat down where he had been before and said, "you are not going to believe what I have just been told?" From the top bunk Bill said.

"He has just phoned his wife to tell her about Sally," with complete shock on his face Bob said.

"How do you?" And before he could finish his girlfriend said from her armchair.

"And he wants a divorce."

"How did you?" Bob stopped and thought, then continued, he pointed at them both and said, "you've both been listening at the wall, haven't you?"

"They are paper thin," smiled his roommate.

"And it does help," put in Sam, "if you use one of these," the two would be spies both held a glass up each.

*

"Well done gentlemen, you have done really well," Kim had joined Bob and Karl in the latter's office at his request to be informed that the night before, security had broken up the fist fight that had been organized for a lot of money to exchange hands. Karl had put one of his men in there once they knew where it was to be held, in one of the drying rooms. All of the lockers had been moved back, at nine o'clock the previous evening.

Karl's man worked out who the main instigators were and the fighters, six in all, there were to be two fights. They had all been sacked and the rest who had been in attendance had been given final written warnings.

"Do I want to know how you came across the information?" Asked the project coordinator. The other two looked at each other then Karl said.

"Kim to be blunt, we felt you tied our hands a little, no a lot." The project coordinator went to talk, but Karl put his hand up and said, "please Kim, let us explain. We knew how much you wanted to stop the gambling and we agreed with you, and that Tim chap did deserve to go, so we came up with another way to find out where the fight was. Notices have now gone up in all areas this morning saying gambling will not be tolerated in any form and my men have been told breakup any gambling they see, anywhere.

"There will always be some form of gambling here Kim," the committee chairman put in, "but this has gone a long way to stop it, if it does not stop it all together it will defiantly slow it down."

"And I am so pleased with what you have both done. I am not going to push you on how you got the information," he thought for a minute then said. "I had a very good friend kill himself a few years ago over gambling, he lost the family home through gambling, his marriage broke up, it was awful. So, I have very strong feelings about this sort of thing." He stood up followed by the other two, shook both their hands and said, "well done again gentlemen," turned and left the office. When he was well out of ear shot Bob smiled and said to Karl.

"Well Karl you've got a hundred and fifty quid left, we could have a little bet with that!"

Chapter 7

Ever been had?

Work was moving on well in all areas, in August 1985. A lot of the temporary roads were now closed with the new ones open. Lorry loads of windows and external doors could be seen on the backs of lorries headed for office buildings and warehouses that were being fitted out internally with partitions forming the work areas within. Lights could be seen shining as work continued late into the evenings.

With the airfield open, aeroplanes were coming in more frequently and while work was still on going around the hangar a date in late August had been agreed for the last Kenya to dock at West Cove. The bridge head would still be used as cargo ships would continue to arrive for the main project and materials for other companies that had been awarded contracts and were now opening up in different areas.

*

"Well done on getting Bill a free phone call home Bob," said Sam as he sat next to her in the armchair in his room after he had made them both teas.

"Yeah I just hope it sorts it for him, with his problem and all," he replied.

"Do you realise it will be just over two months and we will be out of here, on holiday, then on to Algeria," smiled Sam.

"I have a few things to talk to you about, before him on the top bunk gets back," he pointed.

"We can go to my room."

"Oh, I want to see how things have gone with his phone call first." He stood up and walked to his wardrobe which was at the right-hand side of the rooms entrance door, he then opened one of the two doors and took a A4 white envelope off one of the shelves and held it in the air and said. "I got this today," then put it back and returned to the armchair, then continued, "it's the Decree Absolute for my divorce, I can't believe it."

"Oh, Bob," she held his hand, "are you okay?"

"Oh, I just don't know, I mean, I came out here a married man to buy our house, and now, well, I will finish single." Sam kissed on his cheek.

"Bob you know I am here to help you through all of this."

"I know, and I am so grateful to have you." He turned to her and kissed her on the lips. "I think it's the girls above everything, I really miss them, being here and all, but now I won't have them all the time when I am home."

"Bob we will be taking them on holiday soon, and I can't wait to meet them."

"Yes, I have told Jane we are taking them, she is fine, I think she is looking forward to a break, properly bugger off somewhere with that tosser John." Sam squeezed his hand, "I write to the girls all the time."

"Well Mr English, I have news."

"What?"

"I have sorted the holiday out, for the dates you said."

"Oh, right, can I ask where we are going Miss Crisp?"

"I would love it to be a surprise for you."

"Right, aha, what about money etc?"

"We can sort that when we get home, I do trust you," she kissed his cheek again, "then it's off to North Africa."

"That's one of the things I want to talk to you about."

"You haven't changed your mind, have you?" She almost held her breath.

"Nooo, no, not at all, it's you."

"How?"

"You're a woman."

"Oh, you have just noticed," smiled Sam.

"Oh, I have noticed Miss Crisp, yes I've noticed. No, seriously, I have been thinking about how women are treated in some countries like that, women are not in control as a rule, telling people what to do, like you would be."

"We did talk about that at the interview. On the sites there will be local workers but there will also be a lot of British workers and all the managers will be British, and of course I will have you to protect me Mr English," the safety officer smiled and squeezed his hand again.

"Well, up until now it has been you protecting me."

"The thing is you're right, there will be things as a woman I take for granted and I will be aware of that, I will have to keep my head covered at times, and there will be times when I will have to be seen and not heard."

"Can you do that?" Smiled Bob.

"It might not be easy at times" she laughed, "but again that's why I will have you with me. It is another challenge for me. It has been hard at times, telling some men they are not working safely, but I am looking forward to it so much."

"But it's you who speaks the lingo, not me."

"I will teach you French Mr English." Before another word could be spoken the door burst open to reveal Bill who snarled.

"No fucking fags in the shop, sorry Sam. Can't you take up smoking again Bob?" He made his way across the room to his top bunk throwing his blue jacket on the floor as he went.

"Oh, they are running out of everything, with the dock strike in the UK and the Kenya not back for a while," said Sam, "they have run out pads also."

"Pads?" Asked the new comer as he laid down, "what pads, brake pads?"

"Women's things," put in Bob.

"Ugh," growled Bill.

"How did the phone call go?" Asked Bob, as he and Sam got up to leave. Bob then picked up the newcomer's jacket and hung it on the back of the door.

"Oh, all's fine, I've paid them back and the wife had already told that tosser to piss off or her brothers would sort him out."

"But you said you had to calm her down or you would have to go home," said Sam.

"Oh yes, well the thing is I may have laid it on a bit thick so that I got a free phone call, and the lad made a mistake and gave me a five-minute card instead of the three-minute one I was meant to have had, so all's good."

"You lied Bill, and made Bob lie for you."

"I didn't know he was lying," protested Bob.

"Well," smiled Bill, "what's the point of having a roommate in the know if you can't get something out of it every now and then. Oh, saying that Sam, your old roommate from Eastham's, she couldn't get me some fags, could she?"

*

Bob and Sam were sat in their usual positions in the Land Rover with Ed driving, they were on their way back from the quarry, with most of the blasters going sick new ones were being trained up to carry out the work, so the safety officer and the committee chairman had been asked to make sure everything was in place correctly, but Bob had said.

"I wouldn't have a clue how to set a charge, we could all end up getting fucking blown up!" But that did not happen as they had written instructions from one of the blasters on the sick and all had gone well with the new blasters. The operation had to be carried out as JLB was now supplying the other contractors on the island with concrete so the need for stone was very important.

"What's that?" Asked Ed as he pointed over the steering wheel in front of them, as they rounded a bend in the road. Some distance ahead of them a worker was standing in the road beside a lay-by that was used to store three-foot diameter by six-foot-long concrete drainage pipes, behind that was a barbed wire fence with a field that had sheep grazing in.

A 360deg digger was loading the pipes on the back of a tipper lorry. In the road in front of them was one of the workers waving his arms for them to stop, the Land Rover pulled up behind the lorry, the three newcomers all got out of the vehicle. At the back of the lorry were another two workers, one was holding his right-hand in his left-hand, blood could be seen around the hand and on the ground. "He has cut his fingers off," shouted Joe Johnston the forty-year-old Yorkshireman as they approached the workers.

"Okay," said Bob, "I am sure it's not that bad, you must have just caught them Kevin, I know it will feel bad, we have a first aid kit in the Rover, please get it Ed, we will soon sort you out, let's have a look." Kevin Johnston Joe's brother removed his left hand to exposé a fingerless right hand covered in blood with only a thumb remaining. "Shit, fuck," said Bob, "you've cut your fucking fingers off."

"I told you that," replied Joe.

"We've got to get him down to the medical centre," put in Ed.

"Where's his fingers?" Asked Sam.

"Don't know," replied Joe, "they must be on the back of the lorry," he pointed at the rear of the truck that was half loaded with pipes, he caught them between the pipes as they were swinging, took them clean off." Bob ran off to the Land Rover.

"Oh shit," said Ed as he held his own right-hand fingers as if to protect them.

"Let's find them," said Sam, "they may be able to get them back on."

"I'll have a look," said Joe, he went and climbed on the back of the truck as Bob returned with the first aid kit and went about dressing the injured hand. "I can't see them," shouted Joe, they must have fallen between the pipes, it would take a while to unload them again."

"No," said Bob, "let's get him to the medical centre, you radio in Sam and we will get him over there."

"Ok, will do," she walked down the road then after a short while returned and said, "let's go, they are sorting a helicopter out and they will get him on this afternoon's Herc back to the UK." The four got in the land rover and headed for the compound.

*

"The thing is," said Pat O'Conner the forty-one-year-old tubby five-foot-six-inch tall balding, mobile crane driver from North London, "they want to see the letter in which my wife says she is on the brink of a break down and does not know how it will go if I do not come home." He sat with Bob in the office that the committee man used from time to time. "They can get fucked, nosey bastards, what do bloody welfare get some sort of kick out of reading other people's letters, bloody wankers!"

"Well the thing is Pat they have been caught out a few times, if you want compassionate leave they have to check everything out."

"What, don't you believe me?"

"No, I didn't say that," Bob rubbed his chin and said, "look would you let me see it, then I can tell Welfare."

"Oh, fuck it," Pat stood up, "forget it, I'll just fucking jack!"

"Pat, sit down, please," Pat returned to his seat, "I am here to help you, I don't want you to resign and lose loads of money when you have got problems at home."

"Well, they just piss me off, if one of them had issues at home they would soon be out of here."

"Right Pat," they both stood up and shook hands, "leave it with me and I will see what I can do."

*

"What, they are taking work gear home to sell?" Bob asked Karl as they sat in the latter's office drinking tea.

"Yes, it seems like it, I got tipped off from an old mate in the Met, his mate who works in customs at Heathrow told him, they had found a few suitcases full of work gear, a lot of the work clothes were still in the plastic bags."

"How do they get hold of them, we only get our first lot when we get here then we have to hand in the worn-out items to get new ones."

"I know Bob, I think someone who works in the stores must be getting them out of there then selling them to lads, for them to sell when they are on leave or finish, I haven't told Kim yet, he won't be pleased."

"I would say he will be really pissed off."

"Yeah, that's one way of putting it."

"What do you want from me?" Asked Bob as he started to get up.

"Just listen out for any info please, I need to stop this as soon as I can!"

"Oh okay, you don't want me to get you a new jumper and trousers then?"

*

"I heard today," said Bill, as he sat on his top bunk bed while Bob handed out tea to their visitors, Sam and Ed who were in the two armchairs, "that it was all a setup, Kevin the pipe layer, about his fingers being cut off and all."

"No way," said Bob as he sat on his bottom bunk, "I saw his fingers, well saw where they should have been, they had been cut off alright, believe me."

"Oh," continued Bill, "they had been cut off alright, but not here, not that day."

"What do you mean?" Asked Sam.

"I have been told he lost them well over two years ago, in an accident very much like what they said happened here, and he got compensation from the other company. Then came out with his brother and set this scam up."

"I don't believe it," put in Ed, "there was blood everywhere." There were nods of agreement from the other two.

"Sheep's blood, I was told they killed one from a nearby field, then buried the dead sheep with the digger."

"There were sheep nearby to be fair," answered Ed.

"No, no way," continued Bob, "I saw the open ends, ugh, it was horrible."

"They opened the ends up for everyone to see, okay then, did you see the fingers?"

"Yes," said Bob.

"No, we didn't," put in Sam, "his brother said they must have been under the pipes in the lorry and couldn't find them."

"Now that's another thing," the storyteller continued, "his brother jacked and went on the Uganda a couple of days after. I was told that they had it all set up for when you had passed them and knew you would be coming back that way, who better to witness it all than the trusted safety officer and committee chairman and Ed, who no one trusts, joke Ed, joke, before you say anything."

"Ugh."

"Then they put a claim in for compo from this lot."

"No," the chairman said, "there are just too many lies and rumours going on here, how would he have got through the medical, that would have been spotted?"

"Not if it was anything like my medical," put in Ed, "it was like herding cattle, can you bend, can pick things up, ok you can go, I think you could keep your hand out of the way you know."

"Who told you?" Asked the safety officer.

"Sorry," the reply came, then Bill touched the side of his nose, "must keep that to myself or I won't get any more info."

"No, I am not having it, this is another wind up," said Bob as he picked his tea cup off the coffee table and took a sip.

"You did in fact say to me once, that in the time you have been here, there was nothing you would disbelieve now," Sam reminded Bob.

"I just don't know, yes Sam you're right, but this really seems far-fetched."

"Well there is one thing," said Bill from above, "this Kevin could become a thief, burglar or robber now."

"How do you mean?" Asked Ed from the armchair.

"Well, he could rob anywhere he likes, there won't be any fingerprints will there?" Laughed the joke teller from his high position.

*

Bob very rarely drank in mid-week, it had been a rule of his since he had been in the Falklands which overall, he had kept to, but he had been talked into going out this Monday evening as it was the night before the Kenya left West Cove for the last time. He and Sam had eaten on their own later, as they had been delayed getting back from meetings and had agreed to meet their friends in the New Gull & Penguin.

It was already fairly packed with a party atmosphere when they arrived and made their way through the crowd to join Bill, Ed, Reg, Colin, Sally and Wolfie at the large round table that they were waiting at, with beer at the ready for the newcomers. After a short while of chatting Sally said to Colin, "go on," she gave him a nudge in the side with her elbow, "tell him."

"Hmm, well."

"Go on."

"What is it?" Asked Sam

"Well," again Colin found it hard to find the words when Sally said.

"You're useless my man, there's a few things. I am pregnant, Colin's divorce is on the way, and when it's done, we are going to get married, then go and live in Scotland."

"Bloody hell," said Wolfie, "you know how to shock someone lass." Sam got out of her seat and moved around the table to hug Sally. Everyone was shaking Colin's hand and wishing him well, Bob was the last to do this.

"What do you think?" Colin asked his lifelong friend.

"Colin, I can't say much as my marriage is over, look, I just hope it all works out for you."

"Thanks mate." This was interrupted by a very drunk Pat O'Conner who came up behind where Bob was sitting and put his hands on his shoulders, making the committee man jump.

"Thanks Bob," he slurred his words, and Bob turned around to face him, "I am out of here tomorrow."

"Well I am just glad I could help Pat."

"It's great," Pat continued, "I get out of this shithole, I go to the doc I know when I get home, pay him a few quid for a letter to say I am not fit to come back, so I get a medivac and paid up my con-trick, and I've got a suitcase full of work gear off Mickey the storeman to flog when I get home," at this point he nearly fell over but held onto the back of Bob's chair, "and on top of all that," he laughed, "no twat took the time to look at my file to see I am not even married!!!"

Chapter 8

The end of an era.

"You are joking?" Bill greeted the news of Bob and Sam going to work in Algeria with complete surprise and shock, "what the two of you, together, not coming back here, I mean again, ever, after this month?"

"Yes Bill, never again," Bob smiled as he sat in his room in the armchair next his girlfriend holding her hand drinking tea with the other as he looked up at Bill on his top bunk.

"Bloody hell," came the reply, "and I have just signed another six fucking month con-trick, sorry Sam."

"Well," Sam put in, "Ed reckons he's going to spend the rest of his life here paying off his ex-wife's debts, so you can have him move in."

"Yes, we have got to tell him yet," continued Bob, "you are the first one we have told, Bill, we haven't even told Colin yet."

"Oh," replied the voice from above, "he's off also, up there," he pointed to the ceiling, "to Jockland, having babies, shooting the haggis, dancing with cabers or whatever they do up there," he pointed up again, the two listeners both laughed at this.

"Evening everyone," the door opened to the room to show Ed who then walked in, "any tea?"

"Yes," said Bob as he got up, "sit here, I will make it." The two exchanged places and Bob went about his duties.

"Come on," said Bill, "tell him, he won't be happy."

"Not happy, not happy about what?" Asked the new comer.

"Well," said Bob, but before he could say anymore Bill continued.

"They're off, the two of them, pissing off to fucking Africa, sorry again Sam, leaving us here in this shithole."

"WHAT?"

"We were going to tell you in the morning Ed," the safety officer put in.

"Told ME first," he pointed to himself, "I am not happy, just signed up for another six months and they are bloody off to lay on bloody beach's in the fucking sun shine, sorry Sam."

"What's happening, what's happening?" Asked a now stressed looking Ed.

"Well," said Bob, as he handed Ed a cup of tea, "IF BILL," he shouted, "shuts his mouth for one minute I'll explain. We have got a new job in Algeria, North Africa, we." Before he could continue Ed said.

"WHEN ARE YOU GOING?"

"End of this month," put in Bill.

"Shit, fuck, sorry Sam, I've got to stay here forever to pay that bitch's debts, and you're clearing off and leaving me, this isn't good, and you told him up there first," he pointed at Bill who poked his tongue out at him. "Who am I going to be given to work with?"

"You might actually have to do some work now," laughed Bill.

"Piss off," came the reply from a very despondent looking Ed.

"You'll be fine," Sam rubbed his arm, "you can move in with Bill."

"DO I HAVE TO?" This brought laughs from everyone apart from Bill who poked his tongue out again.

"Well Colin goes next month," Bob told him, "and just to cheer you both up a little I will leave you my kettle and radio."

"I can't believe you are leaving us," said a shocked Ed.

"I know," came the voice from above again, "they don't care about us, off to the bloody sun shine, leaving us here."

"Right," said Bob, walking over to Sam and without notice he pulled her out of the armchair by her left arm, "we are off out, see you two later," the two left the room without another word, once in the corridor Bob turned to Sam and said, "that went bloody well then!"

*

Bob and Sam had spent the last hour or so, that bright, but of course windy morning walking together around 'Section 41', which had the newest section manager on the project, Wolfie. They had both been very impressed with the progress, the cleanliness, the safety and the seemingly happy workforce, so it was with happy news that they were about to join the section manager in his office for tea, leaving their driver Ed beside the Land Rover smoking and saying things like.

"I am going to be here forever paying that fucking bitch's debts off," and "I am going to be totally on my own now," or "can you believe I've got to live under Bill, blowing and farting all night." Bob and Sam had these sorts of comments for the twenty minutes since they had left the camp.

"Come in," smiled Wolfie as he welcomed the two visitors from behind his desk, ``just made you both teas," he pointed to the two cups on the desk by the two chairs, they both thanked him as they sat down.

"Well," started Sam, "it looks good out there Wolfie, in a short time as well."

"Thanks Sam, but to be fair I have had lots of help, and all the lads got on side once that tosser Don went, and your nose looks a lot better these days Bob."

Bob rubbed his healed nostrils, his eyes had also almost lost the blackening, then said, "you have done really well big man."

"Oh, and I have got to thank you Bob, and I got a big lump of extra cash this month, and I know you sorted it."

"Not a problem, you deserve it, look Wolfie, we, hmm, Sam and I have some news to tell you."

"Okay, I've got news also, but let me guess, you're having a baby."

"Nooo!" Came the joint reply.

"You're getting married." This was followed by the same reply.

"Look Wolfie, you go first, tell us your news, please?" Bob asked.

"Okay, it's big news," he held his two hands out wide to express the size, "I've got a new job, I am going to North Africa, Algeria." The two-visitor looked at each other as Wolfie asked? "Come on then, what's your news?" They looked at each other again and said together.

"We have got a new job, we are going to North Africa, Algeria!!" There was silence in the office until it was broken by Wolfie who said.

"Fuck off, sorry Sam, you're on a fucking wind up, sorry again Sam."

"No, it's true," smiled the female safety officer, "we leave here at the end of the month, then we're having a holiday with Bob's girls, then we are off to North Africa, Algeria. We will be travelling all over the country so we will see you at some point, no doubt."

"Ok, two things, where are you going on holiday and are you going to be okay Sam, as a woman in Algeria?"

"I would like answers to both of them?" Put in Bob.

"Right," came the reply from Sam, "firstly Bob does not know where we are going for our holiday and secondly being a woman over there, I have got Bob to protect me." She smiled at her boyfriend.

"You're the one who looks after him," laughed the manager.

"Thanks, Wolfie, MATE!" Growled Bob. Before another word could be exchanged between the two males Sam said.

"Everything will be fine," she patted Bob on the knee then continued, "Wolfie, what role are you going out there as, is it a manager?"

"No, it's a charge-hand, I am not saying I will not be a manager again but I put in for the job when I was on leave, I am here a month longer than you two, a month at home then I am off, before her at home can get me to change the kitchen," he laughed.

Before another word could be spoken a worker walked in the office past the counter that Wolfie had now had the door removed from and said, "Boss, I have just found these in the drainage dig," he held his hands out to show a hand grenade in each of them.

"SHIT!" Shouted Bob, jumping up as he saw the objects.

"It's okay, sit down Bob lad, put them in the water bucket with the rest of them Johnny." The tall ginger haired worker turned and left the office.

"Jesus wept Wolfie, they're bloody grenades," barked Bob.

"Don't worry lad," smiled the section manager, "I know how to sort them," he sipped his tea, "found them all the time when we were rebuilding Vietnam after the war there!"

*

"Well I am going to tell Bob now, that you are both leaving," Ed told Sam as they waited in the Land Rover for him to finish a meeting at the Tank Farm, "I mean, me and you, the two of us, you know."

"No Ed, I don't know, what the hell are you on about?" Asked Sam in a surprised tone.

"Us, being asked to spy on him and all."

"Oh, that, well go on then, he's coming," she pointed forward to Bob who was making his way out of David's office with files under his arm. The committee chairman walked over not looking very happy, Ed had already started the vehicle, when Bob was safely in he reversed away from the car park in front of the offices as Bob said.

"That David bloody Antony is nothing but an arrogant tosser, I am so pleased I will have little more to do with him soon, he just thinks he's God's gift."

"I know," said Sam, "he tried," realising she had not mentioned it to Bob, she cut herself short.

"Tried what?" Asked Bob.

"Oh nothing."

"You can't do that, you started, you have got to finish, we don't have secrets, do we Sam?"

"No, we don't Bob, he asked me out the other week, I didn't want to upset you."

"He is a tosser."

"I got something to say also," said Ed as they passed through the Lay Down Area.

"Oh God," smiled Bob, "he didn't try it on with you also Ed?"

"Nooo, it's me and Sam?"

"BLOODY HELL, where is this all going?" Bob asked in a now very shocked voice.

"No Bob," said Sam as she patted his knee, "let him explain, go on Ed."

"Well," said the driver as he concentrated on the road, "George always wanted me to, well, you know."

"Spy on me?"

"Well, I am not sure if spying is the correct term?"

"It will do, Ed I always guessed that, that's why I always kept a lot of things to myself, not that I didn't trust you, well the fact is I didn't know you at first, but as I did get to know you, I didn't want you to be put on the spot."

"There's more," cut in Sam, "Ed and I have both been asked in recent months, by Arran Jones since the Eastham's chap got caught in your room, going through your books."

"Right!"

"I told him to get stuffed," she continued.

"Why didn't you tell me?"

"She said," Ed put in, as he pointed at Sam, "depending which Bob English at the time we told, one could want to out think them, and another one would storm into the office, and tell them to poke their job where the sun doesn't shine."

"Thanks Ed," the safety officer looked sideways at the driver. "Ed's right Bob, neither of us wanted that, did we Ed," the driver nodded his reply. "There was a lot going on at the time, for you, mentally here and your divorce, we really didn't want to put more pressure on you." Bob looked out the window thinking of what he had just heard and after a short while he replied.

"Sam, I am not happy."

"Oh, I am really sorry Bob, I really just wanted to help you," she rubbed his knee. Bob turned and smiled at her and said.

"When I say I am not happy, it's because I have known you just a year or so, and you know me inside out already. Yes, at that time I think I would have told them to poke it. It doesn't surprise me, they always want to keep on top but thanks for telling me, if it didn't drop Ed in it I would make something up to leave them with."

"It's not a problem," said the driver, "I can just say I overheard you."

"Ok, leave it with me."

"There is one other thing you might as well know, now that we are going to see Benjamin and we are just about finished here." Replied Sam.

"Oh, bloody hell," said the committee chairman, "what's this then, it is really bombshell day!"

"I think the reason Kim put us together was for us to fall for each other and you would come back for another contract." Bob thought about this again and said.

"Well," he held her hand, "I suppose that did happen, but while he may have had different reasons, it is one time here I don't mind being used." Their lips came together and exchanged a kiss. "But he did not expect us both to be disappearing off to Algeria," he laughed.

"Yeah," put in Ed as they approached April Ridge, "may I add, I am not sure if I have mentioned this, but leaving me here to pay off that fucking, sorry Sam, bitch's debts."

"You may have just mentioned it a time or two," smiled Sam, "now concentrate on the road Ed," she pointed to how close he had come to being on the wrong side of the road and going close to the drop down the ridge.

"SORRY!" He pulled back across the road, much to the relief of his two passengers. "If we had gone over the edge then, that would have been that bitch's fault as well." They decided not to mention anything else that may wind their driver up. So, it was in silence that they drove the last few miles to the main compound and their meeting with the project coordinator apart from mumbles from Ed mainly referring to, "that fucking bitch!"

*

"So that's it then, I can't talk you into staying?" Asked Kim Benjamin as he sat across the meeting rooms large polished table. Unlike when the office complex first opened, all of the walls in the meeting room were now adorned with progress photos of the project thus far, from the MV Adventure first docking in West Cove up until the first flight landing at the airfield.

Coffee was being drunk by the three occupants of the room in which Bob and Sam later agreed was a very relaxed atmosphere. "I have to say Sam, I am a little surprised you are leaving Johnsons after all these years."

"The thing is Kim, I am still young but I know how fast the years go past, and some opportunities may not come around again, and I have to say coming here has given me the travel bug, working with lads who have worked around the world, like yourself," she pointed at him.

"I dare say there will always be a job back with Johnsons when you're ready, and you know there's another six-month contract on the table for both of you here should you change your minds." There came a joint, "thank you," from the two.

"But that's not going to happen, is it?" The two looked and smiled at each other then again said together.

"No!"

"We are off on holiday with my two daughters," Bob continued, "then it's off to Algeria."

"Where are you going on holiday? Asked the coordinator.

"I don't know, Miss Crisp has sorted it all out and I have not been told yet."

"Soon," she patted his knee.

"Well," said Kim as he got up and walked around the table towards them both with his hand out to shake theirs, "I know things have not always been easy at times here, but I believe it could have been a lot worse, and I have you to thank you for that Bob, well done," they shook hands. "I would like to have a drink with you both before you go next week."

"Not a problem," said Bob as they shook hands, Kim hugged Sam and kissed her on her right cheek. The two left the meeting room and walked along the corridor in silence towards the exit to the car park and the waiting Ed when Sam said after looking behind herself.

"Bob, do you think he is as bad as we have thought he is?" They stopped and looked at each other and the male said, after thinking for a few moments.

"Sam, Benjamin is a total control freak, his only goal being here is to make sure the company comes out on top, that's what he is here for. I don't dislike him, because that's what he is paid for, but I think he is totally over the top at times. Do I trust him? No, I wouldn't trust him as far as I could throw him, and that wouldn't be far." Bob fell silent then said, "would I put him out if he was on fire?" He laughed and said, "I might piss on him, to put him out. Yes, I might enjoy that!"

*

Bob, Sam, Bill, Ed and Wolfie were all sitting together at nine-thirty on the first two's last Sunday morning on the island eating breakfast with their friends in the large canteen, sat next to the window wall that had the spring sun shining through.

The talk was the usual shit as Bill had put it in the past, when Wolfie asked about all of the things that Bob had just recently found out about.

"I know," Bob replied, "but these two kept them from me, to stop me from getting upset, I am okay with that."

"Well," said Bill with a mouth full of scrambled egg spitting out everywhere, "and the biggest surprise was finding out that the wife was getting shagged while you were out here, I always said." Before the man from Birmingham could say another word, Sam pointed at him and said in a loud and angry voice.

"We all know what you have said BILL, we don't need to hear it again, so just SHUT THE FUCK UP!" Silence fell around the table as everyone looked at Sam in complete shock, then at that precise moment one of the last Erect-A-Com employee's still working on the project came running in and shouted out.

"Everyone, quiet please," he put one finger to his lips, there was mumbling still, so to make the point he shouted, "FUCKING SHUT UP!!" Then after a few seconds he said, "please?" The almost full canteen sat in silence looking at the tall twenty-eight-year-old newcomer who continued by saying, "all will be revealed very soon, when I give the word, I want you all to shout out, WAKE UP YOU PISS HEAD." It was soon after that six silent co-workers of the first person walked in with three on each side carrying the top section of a bunk bed, with a very fast asleep and snoring bearded face large forty-year-old worker laying on his back. The first worker had cleared a breakfast table which the bed was placed upon for everyone to see, Joey who had done this, then for everyone to see held his hand in the air then showed one finger, then two, as he showed the third the whole canteen shouted as one.

"WAKE UP YOU PISS HEAD!" Davy, the up until now unconscious worker, sat upright showing off his bare hairy chest, to great roars of laughter from everyone but himself.

"WHAT the fuck?" He asked as he took the scene in around him after he had wiped his eyes with the back of his hand.

"What was the last thing you said to me last night, when you woke me up when you came in pissed out of your head, as you are every Saturday night?" Asked his roommate Joey.

"I don't know," came the reply, "I was pissed."

"As you nearly fell on me, you said, 'Joey, don't let me miss breakfast tomorrow, I miss breakfast every Sunday, get me up'. Well mate we got you up, okay?" Not many could hear Davy as the laughter was so loud, but Joey heard his roommate say to him.

"You fucking wanker!"

*

"Ok Mr English, what is the big surprise? Or did you just want to get me back to my room, on my own, for a Sunday morning kiss and a cuddle?" Smiled the safety officer as they sat in the two armchairs in her room after returning from the canteen after breakfast.

"No, it's not for that Miss Crisp," then after thinking for a moment he continued, "well I won't rule that out later," he smiled.

"Come on you bugger," she punched him on the arm, "the suspense is killing me."

"Well, sometime ago you said to me, that you felt after your Dad died and you split up with Robbie, you felt mentally that you were sort of in a wilderness."

"I DID! You remember that?"

"I do, and with my split up from Jane and everything, I have thought about it, and well, I could say the same about myself," he squeezed her hand then took some paper out of his in-side jacket pocket and continued, "I have written you a poem." He unfolded the paper, Sam snatched it out of his hand and started to read.

The Wilderness.

How long had I been walking in this wilderness?
I don't know, weeks or months? It had been a long time.

The hot gritty burning sand below my bare feet, rocks that cut and the yellow ball in the sky that burned my back.
I had come across oasis and had the odd rest.
I met other people, we chatted then went our different ways.
I knew I had to keep going, to where I was not sure, but to stop for too long would be to give up and that I could not do.
Vultures were above me in the sky just waiting for me to fall, so keep going I did.
For many miles I kept walking mainly with my head hung low.
Then one day out of the blue I looked up and saw you in front of me.
I' am not sure what made me think you were the right person to walk with, was it the smile, the pretty face the happy chat, I don't know maybe all, but right I knew it was.
We stopped and talked, laughed and had some fun, before I knew it we had started to walk together.
The walking was still not easy, but now I knew that if I tripped over a rock I had you to help me up.
We walked for many miles and as we shared our fears and worries of being in the wilderness alone, the journey became easier.
Was it the helping hand we gave each other, or was it the arm around the shoulder, or just knowing we were there for each other.
Wrapped up in our joy for the other, we did not notice at first but the hot sand had turned to soft cool grass below our bare feet.
We stood and looked at the town before us, was this the end of our journey together?
As we looked into each other's eyes we knew the answer.
Good things should not come to an end, if it can be helped.
No, this was now the start of a new journey, together, on into and beyond the town to take up new challenges that lay before us, together!

Bob English.

October 1985.

Sam wiped tears from her eyes then turned to Bob and gave him a long passionate kiss then said, "I love you Bob English, so much, and I love the poem, it's beautiful, thank you so much."

"Well you gave me the inspiration to talk about being in the wilderness, I've been working on it for some time now, I wanted to complete it before we left here."

"Bob, I love it."

"After you had said that to me, I thought about when we first met, and while I was still married and everything was all right with Jane, or so I thought. I was struggling here and, well you helped me so much, and thinking back since we have known each other, before we became aha."

"Lovers?" Sam prompted him.

"Yes, but we did help each other along, and now I see that so much."

"We met at a time that was right for both of us Bob, sometimes things happen like that, even if we did have to come to the other side of the world to meet."

"You're right, you have really helped me since the split up and everything, really been there for me, that's why I wanted to do the poem, for you Sam."

"Bob English, I think it's time for that kiss and cuddle."

*

"I don't mind if you don't tell me where the holiday is, but I do need to know how much I owe you, money wise?" Bob asked his girlfriend as they made their way across the open area from the accommodation to meet their friends in the bar the night before they left the Island for the last time.

"Bob please don't worry about the money, you have got enough to worry about, having to pay for the girls and other things, PLEASE," she pleaded as they stopped and looked at each other.

"Sam, you can't pay for it, I won't let you." Came the reply from Bob.

"OK, you owe me two thousand pounds, now, cash," she held her hand out.

"BLOODY HELL, where in God's name are we going?"

"I am joking," smiled the mischievous safety officer, "we are going to Greece, a small holiday resort, I have got us a family room so the girls are in with us. It will still be warm given its October, and regarding the money, I have a friend who owns a travel agency, she has sorted us a good deal, so please forget about the money, let's," she kissed him on the lips, "let's go and enjoy our last night here, ever!"

"Will you ever do anything I ask you?" The male replied as they started walking again.

"No, I doubt it," came the smiling reply, as they walked into the entrance of the recreation centre then headed towards the large bar at the left-hand end of the walk way, where they had agreed to meet their friends. Before they entered the bar, Sam stopped and turned to Bob and said with a smile on her face, "you can pay me off in kind Mr English," then continued into the bar.

Wolfie, Bill, Ed, Reg, Colin and Sally were already sitting around the round table with beers ready for the newcomers. Greetings were exchanged as everyone sat down in what was becoming a very packed, noisy and boisterous bar.

"Well that's it," said Wolfie across the table in a loud voice to the newcomers, "you've done your last day in this shithole?"

"Yes," came the reply from the now ex-committee chairman, "this time tomorrow we should be in a hotel at home," he turned and smiled at his girlfriend with whom he was holding hands.

"Better than two weeks on that old rust bucket of The Kenya," put in Colin.

"Oh, I really wanted to go on it," put in Sam.

"Believe me," said Bill, "you wouldn't be on it long and you would have wished you had flown."

"It can't be worse than the Air Bridge," the female replied.

"Oh," said Reg, "at least with that it's over after twelve hours or so, not wandering around for two weeks with sod all to do."

"So, we will meet up in Algeria," smiled Wolfie.

"Yes," replied Bob, "oh bloody hell," he choked on his beer as a group of swaying, drunken workers backed into him.

"Give them a thump," said Ed, as he moved to one side to stop them bumping into him.

"Yes," smiled Bob, "it would be a fitting way to finish here, with a punch up on the last night that is."

"Bloody hell," said Bill, looking beyond Bob and Sam, "look what the cat dragged in." They all turned to see Kim Benjamin and Arran Jones making their way through the crowd towards them. When they arrived at the table Bob went to stand up, but the project coordinator stopped him by putting his hand on his shoulder.

"Stay there Bob old chap, we will see you in the morning, but we just wanted to pop in tonight, we are not staying but," he grabbed Bob's hand and put something in it, "this is for you all to have a drink and a good night, but don't forget the rest of you are at work tomorrow." The two turned and left as fast as they had entered. Bob looked and four five-pound notes in his hand and said.

"Could someone please pinch me and wake me up."

"Pinch you, I will punch you if you don't go and get the beers in," called out Bill, "before that tight bastard changes his mind and comes back for the money!"

*

"God my bloody head is hurting," Bob said as he sat in the taxiing aircraft next to a window with Sam in the seat beside him the following morning. Sam had not remained in the bar long, she had left her boyfriend with his friends as she still had much to do before leaving, and she did know that things were going to, "get messy," the way the beer was flowing and the fact all the males at the table were not going to leave until they had drunk, "that wanker Benjamin's money."

It was left to Sam to wake Bob up for his last breakfast on the island and she also woke the others up to go to work, and in every case took great joy in making a lot of noise, which brought some very colourful comments from those on the receiving end.

This was followed by breakfast that ended very emotionally with everyone saying goodbye to people they may never see again. The two then made their way to the office compound to say their goodbyes there.

"Well Mr English, if you do drink as if it's the last time you will ever drink again, well the fact is, I have no sympathy for you, WHAT SO EVER!" She shouted the last bit into his ears, which he then covered with both hands. It was at this point that he saw Mickey the storeman walk on to the plane, he had been dismissed for stealing work gear and passing it on to be sold. Bob had passed on the information he got from a drunken Pat O'Conner the night before he left to Karl, as a going away gift. Which the security manager appreciated very much. Bob never liked to see anyone lose their job, but he did think Mickey was taking the piss with the amount of gear he had been selling. Karl had said to Bob that last morning, "I know I will miss all the help you have given me Bob."

The aeroplane moved to the end of the runway and revved up its engines as it prepared itself for take-off, as Bob again covered his ears as Sam said looking out of the window, "do you think we will ever come back here again Bob?" He removed his hands and looked at the now passing airfield then turned to Sam and said.

"After almost two years here and what it has done to my life, I would like to say no, but if I have learned anything in the years I have been on this earth, that is, always to expect the unexpected."

"And," she held his hand, "we would have never have expected you and I," she kissed him on the cheek.

Chapter 9

The Holiday.

"Well it wasn't me who shagged someone I used to go out with," said Bob in an angry voice, but not loud enough for his two daughters to hear, who were waiting in the kitchen for Bob, whom had just arrived to take them on holiday and was talking to his ex-wife in the downstairs hallway.
   "No but you have been having it off with this, whoever she is."
   "Only after you done it, after we split up. We were only workmates before that, she was female, that's all, I wouldn't have gone back for a second contract if things had been good between us, you know THAT!"
   "Oh Bob, I am really sorry," she went to hold his arms but he backed away, "yes you're right, but it's over now, with John, please come home, please," she pleaded, "we have been through too much all these years," she wiped tears from her eyes, "to let a little mistake like this come between us."
   "A little fucking mistake," he growled still in a low voice, he was unable to finish his sentence as the kitchen door opened to show his two daughters in matching pink and white checked dress's their father had brought them that morning.
   "Are we going Daddy?" Asked Lynn, the youngest one. Bob looked at his ex-wife and said.
   "Yes darling, we are going now, I'll get your case's, say goodbye to Mummy please." He picked the two new suitcases he had also purchased for his daughters that morning. Jane kissed and hugged her daughters, and said to them, "have a lovely time, put your sun cream on." Then she turned to her ex-husband with tears running down her cheeks and pleaded again, "Bob, PLEASE!" He looked at her as he headed for the front and snarled.
   "NO!!"

*

"This is Sam, girls," Bob and his two pretty faced long blonde-haired daughters had met Sam at a table in a restaurant in the departure lounge at Gatwick airport, both of them were carrying their toy penguins that Bob had given them.

"Hello," Sam put her hand out to both of them to shake which they did, then they all sat at the square table. "Oh, I love your penguins, I have one also."

"Is yours in your case?" Asked Lynn, as the waiter came up to take their orders, Bob ordered for himself and the girls as Sam pointed to her choice as she said.

"Oh no, Percy, that's his name, is at my home, he is at the end of my bed."

"Is he asleep?" Asked Lynn.

"Well, not really, he lives at the end of my bed. What are the names of your penguins?" Sam asked them both.

"Mine is George," put in Karen, "and Lynn's is Andrew."

"They are into the pop group Wham!" Said their father.

"*Wake me up before you go, go*," sang Sam.

"*Don't leave me hanging on like a yo-yo,*" came the singing reply from the two girls. This brought laughter from the four diners.

"Did you buy your own penguin?" Asked Lynn.

"No," when she had finished she felt she could have chosen her words better, as she said, "your Daddy brought it for me." There was a silence then Lynn asked.

"Do you buy everyone penguins Daddy?" Then Karen continued.

"You didn't buy Mummy one!" Bob and Sam looked at each other, then after another short silence Sam replied.

"Well, your Daddy brought Mummy lots of other things," then quickly changing the subject said, "do you know where we are going on holiday?"

"No," came the joint reply.

"Do you want to know?" Sam continued. "Oh, and by the way I love you matching pink and white dresses."

"Daddy brought them for us this morning," said Lynn.

"You have a lovely kind Daddy, girls," she smiled, "where were we, oh yes, do you want to know where we are going?"

"Yes, yes, yes," came the excited replies.

"Well it is Greece." This drew a blank from both girls.

"It's ok Sam, you can show them the books you have after we have eaten."

"Mummy said," Karen continued, "Sam is a boy's name, you're not a boy, are you?"

"Nooo," came the smiling reply, "I am not a boy, my name is Samantha, Sam is just short for it." Again, this brought a puzzled look from the pair. Bob then said.

"You can tell your bloody MOTHER," in an angry voice, but he was interrupted by his girlfriend, who said.

"You can tell your Mother," smiled Sam, "it is a boy's and a girl's name," she looked at Bob as if to say, "shut up!"

Karen then said, "Mummy said to tell you Daddy, that she still loves you." The two adults both looked at each other but before another word could be spoken.

"Daddy, Daddy," cried Lynn as she jumped off her seat holding herself between the top of her legs as a tray of drinks arrived, "I need a wee-wee, I need a wee-wee, NOW!"

"Oh," said Bob as he started to get up.

"No," said Sam, "you don't want to go to the smelly men's toilet, oh pooh," she held her nose and pulled a face, "come on I will take you, do you need to go Karen?"

"No, but I will come and have a look at the toilets, I like looking at new toilets." The three females got to their feet as Sam held both of the girl's hands and said.

"You enjoy your beer Mr English, us young ladies are off to powdered our nose's." The three turned and walked hand in hand towards the sign with a female in a skirt on it.

*

They were mid-way through their week's holiday in a large family room with a very spacious balcony overlooking the wide golden sandy beach and deep blue sea, which had many small fishing and pleasure boats bobbing around on its clam surface.

Sam's friend Dianna, had picked the room for them. As it was large for a family and the girls had bunk beds that were in one corner which was partitioned off with its own door to make it a separate room within the room, giving the adults in their double bed, extra privacy.

As it was a Sunday, Bob wanted to pay the extra cost and have breakfast on room service which had arrived at nine am, and had been laid out on the large round table on the balcony which overlooked the relaxing view in front of them, with the early morning sun shining the four sat and ate their meal.

"Sam?" Asked Karen as she was finishing her cereal, and without giving her a chance to answer continued, "Mummy said you made Daddy stop smoking."

"Well, I think your Daddy wanted to stop, and I just helped and encouraged him." Before anymore could be said Lynn put in.

"Sam, can you not sleep at night?"

"Yes Lynn, I can, why do you ask?"

"You make a lot of noises at night, and sometimes in the morning as well!" At this point her father

started to choke on his scrambled eggs. Before anymore could be said Karen put in.

"I told you, they are Mummy and Daddy noises Lynn."

"I know, but I have been thinking about that, and Sam is not our Mummy, so why does she make Mummy noises?" At this point Sam put her hand over her mouth to stop herself from laughing as Bob wiped his mouth with a napkin, had a drink of orange juice to clear his throat and said.

"Ok, so what are we going to do today, who wants to go swimming?" The two girls both put their hands in the air and said together.

"Yes please, yes please, yes please."

"Ok," came the reply, "go and get your things ready," the two young ladies jumped down and ran into their sleeping area. "Bloody hell," said Bob, "that's you," as he pointed at the person next to him.

"Well Mr English," she held his hand, "it's you who makes me make Mummy noise's, you bugger," she smiled as she thumped his arm.

*

Sam and Bob sat around a low round table with five armchairs in the lounge bar of their hotel. The children's disco had just finished, and the adult one was due to start in three quarters of an hour. Both events had been advertised for every evening, but this was in fact the first night it had gone ahead since they had been there.

Karen and Lynn had been dancing along with other children on the small dance floor in front of an equally small stage which the disco was set up on, with a mid-twenties, medium height slim blond-haired female DJ from Oxford in England named Susie.

The girls ran back to join the two adults at the table both picking up their lemonades and drinking them very fast. "Slow down," said Bob, "you will make yourselves ill drinking like that."

"Very hot," said Lynn wiping her forehead with the back of her left hand, "it's very hot all this dancing Daddy."

"And you are both very good dancers," a voice said from behind Bob and Sam, the two turned to see Susie standing behind them. "You have got two lovely daughters there," smiled the pretty DJ.

"Thank you," said Bob.

"Daddy is our Daddy but Sam is not our Mummy, but she does make Mummy noises," said Lynn as she took another drink through her straw.

"WHAT?" Asked Susie.

"Yeah," said their father, "let's not go there with that one again."

"You are very good," Sam quickly put in, "sit down and join us," she patted the empty armchair between her and Karen.

"Oh, I was just going to get a drink," came the reply.

"Sit down," said Bob, "I will get you one, what would you like?"

"Oh, thank you," she sat down.

"What would you like?" Asked Bob again as he called a nearby waiter over by rising his arm in the air.

"I would love a small gin with lots of ice and tonic please," she said to the waiter, who nodded his agreement.

"And the same again for us two please," Bob pointed to his and his girlfriends' almost empty glasses.

113

"And us please Daddy?" Said Karen.

"No, you will be going to the toilet all night," came the reply.

"Please, please, please," they both pleaded with their father.

"One more and that's it," he nodded to the waiter.

"There was meant to be a disco every night, but this is the first one," observed Sam.

"We asked," continued Bob, "and they said there was a technical problem."

"Yeah," the DJ replied, "some technical problem," she motioned the two adults to come closer and in a quieter voice continued. "I only got here yesterday, I had just got home to Oxford after a long stint from May in a club in Tenerife. I was going to have a welcome break, when an agent I use sometimes called me and said they needed a DJ here urgently and they would increase my money."

"Extra money is always good," observed the male.

"Yeah, well as I said, I got here yesterday and they picked me up at the airport, and there was a big chap with me all the time, who did just not talk. When I got to the room I was given it was full of women's clothes, make up, everything. I went down to reception and said they have given me someone's room. They said the manager was here now and I had to see him." The drinks arrived at the table and the waiter handed them out, Bob passed him some money, as Susie continued.

"The last DJ, who's room I have got was last seen in a local coffee shop, talking to two old British women, she went off somewhere with them and has not been seen since, that was over a week ago." The storyteller sipped her drink through a straw.

"What has happened to her?" Asked Bob.

She motioned the two back in and in a soft voice continued. "They don't know for certain, but the police said they think the old women are part of a gang that moves around the Mediterranean and these parts, they kidnap young women and they get sold in the Middle East, Africa or Asia to rich people or gangs, as sex slaves."

"Oh, my good god," said Sam in a shocked voice as she then put her right hand to her mouth and leant back in her armchair.

"Bloody hell," said Bob as he took a drink of his beer, "you read about that sort of thing, but bloody hell."

"I have a bodyguard with me every time I leave this place. Just be careful while you are here, I mean all you females, I mean the girls as well, don't leave them anywhere on their own, not the swimming pool or anywhere, I don't think these bastards care about their age or anything like that."

"Shit, sorry ladies," Bob rubbed his chin as he looked at his two daughters now sat in the same armchair laughing and tickling each other.

"Oh, I am sorry to upset you, I just thought you should know."

"Nooo," Bob said, "thanks for telling us, we go the day after tomorrow."

"One of us will be with the girls all the time, and I will not be going anywhere with old ladies," Sam said shaking her head.

"Look," said the DJ as she got up, "I have got to get ready for the next session, thank you for the drink," she held it up, "I will maybe see you tomorrow," they all said their, "goodbyes," as she departed.

"Wow," said Bob after a short silence, "I am not sure what to say about all that," he looked at his daughters again.

"Look Bob, we are only here another couple of days, we never leave the girls on their own, we always go out together, and the truth is a story like that will only put us on our guard."

"Yes, you're right, again," he smiled looking at his girls who were now rolling together on the floor laughing, "oh it's just awful." He shook his head as if in a state of shock.

"The thing is, they will not be hanging around now, they will have moved on, looking for another poor unsuspecting victim."

"It's made me more worried about you being in North Africa now."

"Bob, that's the whole point, now we are on our guard," she held his hand, "I will look after you," he looked at her with a puzzled look, "I don't want you getting dragged off to be someone's sex slave," she smiled, "that's what I want you for. Now let's forget what we have just heard for the time being, get these girls to sleep and then you can make me make some more Mummy noises!"

*

"Karen, Lynn, come back here," their father called out after the girls had run from where they had been playing in a small child's swimming pool, next to the adult's one at the rear of their hotel. Bob and Sam were sitting on sun loungers next to each other, the girls had run to the other end of the outside area to play on a slide.

"BOB, we can still see them," put in Sam.

"I want them HERE!" Came the snapped reply.

"Bob you will freak the girls out if you are not careful."

"Freak them out," he sat up and raised his voice, "that bloody DJ has, FREAKED ME OUT!!"

"Bob," she reached between the beds, "please calm down, we go tomorrow and have had a lovely time, please don't spoil it. I know you're worried, but we have a wall around us and there is only staff and guests here, please relax."

"Oh," he laid back, "I got up in the night and went and checked on them."

"I know, I heard you."

"Daddy, Sam, Daddy, can we go to the bar to get ice cream PLEASE?" Asked Karen as the two girls came and re-joined them.

"No," he sat up again, "I will go," he started to get up.

"You have let us go on our own before," replied Karen.

"I will take them Mr English," Sam got up and pushed him back. "I will get you a beer also, please RELAX!" She bent over and kissed him on the lips, "come on girls, I think it's one cold beer for Daddy and three BIG ice creams for us girls," this was greeted by cheers from the two young ones.

*

"Will we see you again?" Karen asked Sam as the four holiday makers stood together in the arrivals lounge at Gatwick Airport after leaving the aeroplane from Greece.

"Oh yes, I would say so," smiled Sam as she got to her knees to kiss them goodbye.

"Can we all go on holiday again, please," asked Lynn, "I really liked it, not like being with Mummy, moan, moan, moan," she pulled a face and shook her head from side to side, which brought a smile to the two adults' faces.

"I think so," replied the female safety officer, "and Daddy can pay next time!"

"It's a deal," came the males reply.

"Now that Daddy is not married to Mummy anymore," asked Karen, "will you marry Daddy? Lynn and I have talked about it and we would like you as another Mummy, we think it would be nice to have two Mummy's."

"Right, ok," put in Daddy, "it's time to go now girls, we have a train to catch, say goodbye to Sam please." Sam pulled the two girls together as Lynn asked in a soft voice that only the three of them could hear.

"If you do marry Daddy, can we be bridesmaids, please, please, please?"

"Not only will you be bridesmaids," Sam replied in a whisper, "but I will take you out to choose and buy the dresses for you!" This brought a very excited reply from the two girls in the manner of jumping up and down and squealing, she then kissed them both then got to her feet.

"What was all that about?" Asked a puzzled Daddy.

"Girls talk," she tapped her nose, "Mr English, girls talk, I will see you at Heathrow next week," she kissed him on the lips, "don't be late."

Chapter 10

Welcome to the heat.

"What fuck this," shouted one of the airport guards in broken English as he held a small pair of red knickers high in the air that he had just pulled out of Sam's suitcase that he was searching at the North African airport as she and Bob queued to enter the country.

"Give them back," barked the safety officer as she pulled them out of his hand. Sam had a long blue and white flowered patterned dress on with her head covered in a thin light brown linen cloth scarf.

"Nice," smiled the short and very overweight mid forty-year-old customs officer whose blue uniform jacket looked as if it was about to burst open, and his peaked hat looked as if it was ready to fall off the back of his head. Sam pushed the item of underwear back into her suitcase which he had just finished almost emptying on the metal table he was standing behind, he then moved on to Bob whose case was open as he left Sam to repack hers. "Give me knife?" He held out his hand to Bob.

"I haven't got a knife," answered Bob.

"Give me KNIFE!" The guard barked as he repeated his request.

"I don't have ONE," Bob held his hands out in front of him and barked at the officer.

"Go fuck off," the customs man said as he pushed Bob case along the table, then said to the next worker who was waiting with his case open as they had all been instructed to do, "give me knife?"

"Welcome to Algeria," laughed Bob to his girlfriend as he closed his case. The two then moved through the customs hall which had large fans spinning around in the ceiling to keep the area cool, while it was later in the year the temperature was still fairly high. They then queued at passport control to have their passports stamped before moving to the arrival's hall, which was packed with people waiting for passengers off the Friday evening flight from London's Heathrow Airport.

It was Sam who saw the sign with Kingston & Easton on it held high in the air above the crowd by their waiting driver Ken Golding, a twenty-seven-year-old from Sunderland in the north east of England. The two made their way to introduce themselves to the well-tanned stocky medium height driver. After the greetings were made and as soon as they were joined by two more new male workers, they followed Ken out of the front of the terminal and into the dark and heat of the evening. They crossed the grass in the middle of the road to the white minibus which had the companies name embossed in blue on each side which was parked long ways in a parking bay facing the lawn.

In the centre of the worn lawn was a flag pole, which with night time drawing in two males in uniform were removing the national flag which had two equal vertical bars of green and white, in the centre were a red star and crescent, a symbol of Islam, as the nations prominent faith. This flag was adopted on the third of August 1962, after independence from France.

With Sam and Bob in the front seats of the mini bus it was about a twenty-minute drive to the outskirts of the capital at Regama, where a site was under construction and was the base camp for that "stream." There were three streams across the country, each with approximately ten sites of varying size buildings which made up the camps.

As it was almost ten thirty pm when they arrived, they were given a room in a white port-a-cabin in the accommodation area not far from the offices, canteen and bar, not too different from the size they had in the Falklands.

*

It was after breakfast the following morning that the pair made their way to the offices for a meeting they had been informed about by Ken the driver the night before. They were now sitting in a small meeting room around a table, with one other person.

It was discussed about their welcome at the airport the previous evening, but they were told that was "normal here" and that some lads had lots of items taken off them, which were never returned.

"You will sort all of your paperwork, passports, vaccinations, visas etc, with Dave the office manager," the man talking was James Hardwick the stream manager, a very large and heavy man in his forties with very dark black hair, that Sam later told Bob that she thought was "out of a bottle," from Edinburgh in Scotland. "But firstly, I want to explain about the work situation." He took a drink of the tea in front of him then continued. "We have a few problems, I need you here for a while Sam and I need you up at a site about an hour from here at Baran, Bob."

"I was told we would be working together?" Put in the safety office.

"Yes, you will be, but we have a problem at Baran we need to, hmm, let's say, to sort out."

"What's happened? Asked Bob.

"To say it's a long story is an understatement, but I will try to abbreviate it as much as I can.

We had a chap, Peter Hilton on the site who stole and sold one of the site's mobile welding sets to a local builder. But when it came to the bloke paying Peter he refused, as he said it wasn't his to sell."

"That could get a person a good beating where I come from," observed Bob.

"Ah, well yes," James answered, "that's what did happen, and the local went to the police and Peter has been locked up ever since."

"Oh, I don't think I would like to be locked up here," commented Bob.

"Your right," the manager continued, "our company sacked him and well let's say washed their hands on him."

"Well," put in Sam, "if someone steals and breaks the law, of course they will be sacked."

"The thing is," James carried on, "there is no trial date yet and a person has to be fed by their family or friends when in prison here, if not they are on only bread and water."

"Wow," was the shocked reply from the two newcomers.

"We did not take him any food so he was on just bread and water. He has a mate here who was collecting money from the lads to buy him food and he also contacted Peters family in the UK, who went to their MP and said if it wasn't sorted they would go to one of the tabloid newspapers with it. We have now been told by our office in the UK that we have to take him food and drink three times a day, we think it came from the government."

"Where do we come into it?" Asked Bob.

"Our office manager up there, Colin Parker has been taking food to him three times a day, but it is almost taking up the best part of his day by time he gets there, and stays while he eats."

"Can't he just take it all up in the morning?" Asked the safety officer.

"We tried that and he had it taken off him by other prisoners and guards, that's why Colin has to stay while he eats it."

"Bloody hell," said Bob.

"We would like you to take over from Colin, Bob, until it's sorted. Our people at home are pushing to get a date sorted for the trial. We have a driver, a local lad who will take you there each day, you can get the food from the site canteen up there."

"They have heard about your driving," smiled Sam.

"Sod off," came Bob's reply.

"His breakfast has been sorted today. Hamid your driver has been in the prison with Colin so he will look after you. Hamid has got fairly good English so you'll be fine with him, he's a nice chap. Go up there in the mornings, breakfast for eight thirty to nine, lunch midday, take the evening meal at five ish then you can be back here to eat at six ish, your days sorted," smiled James. "Are you okay with all of that Bob?"

"Do I have any choice?"

"Well, let's say you would be helping us all out, a lot"

"No, that's fine," Bob replied, "but what about Sam?"

"We want her to sort some safety paper work here that needs bringing up to date, until this is all out of the way." Sam nodded her reply. "Okay," James got up, "I will give you two a couple of minutes while I go and find Hamid." He left the room.

"Bloody hell, I didn't expect this," Bob said when the door was shut.

"No not at all," came the reply.

"Well I suppose it will be interesting to see what the prisons are like here compared to ours, not that I have been in one of ours, that is."

"Good, well don't get yourself locked up here Mr English," she leant across and kissed him on the lips.

*

By time everything had been completed and Hamid the thirty-five-year-old stocky dark-skinned driver and Bob had got to the site at Barna and met Colin the office manager and collected Peters food it was gone midday, they then made their way up the hill at the other side of the town to the prison. Bob spent most of the time looking out of the window taking in the sights of his new surroundings.

On the journey that morning they had passed much arid landscape, broken by the odd village and hamlet, which were made up mainly of small square white dwellings and shops.

"It seems hotter here Hamid than at the base camp," the passenger observed.

"Yes Mr Bob, it's what you say, higher here and inland, nearer the desert."

"Right," came the reply as the large dirty white van pulled up at the prison gates and Hamid talked to the guard and shook hands this was then followed by them both touching their hearts. The guard then looked in at Bob who smiled back, he then went to the large metal iron railing double gates, he pulled across the large metal bar that kept them together, then pushed them both inwards, the guard then waved the van through.

After they had parked Hamid led the man carrying a middle-sized cardboard box with the prisoner's food within it. The next guard they saw was sitting on a stool at the start of a dimly lit corridor which had six single cells with barred doors and fronts on each side. After the guard had taken out the two cheese and onion rolls which were on top of the box, Colin had told Bob to do this every time they went as it made things a lot easier and stopped the guards from taking Peter's food.

"You must be Bob?" Asked Peter, the gaunt looking five-foot-ten-inch-tall, slim, with black unkept hair and unshaved in shirt and trousers that seemed to be almost falling off him as the two sat on the side of the one bed which had a mattress one blanket and one pillow. Along with a toilet bucket a small glazed barred window this made up the eight-foot-wide by twelve-foot-long brick walled cell.

"Yes," said Bob, as he held the box for Peter to take his food out of along with a flask of freshly made tea. "God it's grim in here," he looked around then said, "bloody hell it pen and inks."

"It's mainly the shit bucket over there," he nodded towards the bucket that had a large group of fly's hovering around it, "they empty it each morning, but to be fair, after six weeks in here I can't smell it."

"Six-weeks, and no trial date?"

"No," sputtered the prisoner, as he ate his roll, "Colin says they just don't know."

"Don't take this the wrong way mate but you look a right mess, can't we get you some new clothes in?"

"I've asked, Colin says they have been told just to feed me. They don't give a fuck about me. But to be fair I nicked the gear then kicked the shit out of the Arab, they just want me to be out of here, I am an embarrassment to them."

"Let me see if I can get some new clothes for you, and get you cleaned up."

"Don't make the gear too good mate, as the guards will take them off you, or rip them off me."

"Well, I will talk to the lads on site, I am sure I can get you some second-hand gear, leave it with me, I will try to sort it out."

"Thanks Bob," he took a drink of tea, "have you got any fag's, ciggie's I am drying for a smoke."

"I don't smoke, packed it up at the start of the year, but as soon as I get my local money allowance I will get some for you."

"Have you got no English money, sterling?"

"Yes, but I have never had a chance to get to a bank yet, we only arrived last night"

"Bloody hell," snarled the eating man, "they only give five or six to one Dinar, get it off one of the Ragheads (the term Ragheads was use by the workers for the locals, many of whom wore turban like head ware) on site, they will give you give you twenty or twenty-five to one."

"Oh," came the surprised reply.

"See what you can do about a trial date as well can you?"

"Look, I can't promise you the world, and you know you cocked up, but that is in the past, I can't believe how you are living. I will do everything I can to make things better for you and try to get you out as soon as possible. But I need a bit of time, I haven't been here a day yet."

"And you have been given this shit to deal with." He wiped his mouth with the back of his hand. Look thanks mate," they shook hands. "I will really appreciate any thing you can do for me," he said in an emotionally charged voice. Bob stayed with Peter until he had consumed all of the food and drink. As he left the prisoner started to do press-ups on the floor. Bob stood outside the cell for a few moments looking at the figure before him on the floor.

Bob then returned to Hamid who was talking to the cell block guard, whom it turned out to be his cousin. They then made their way back to the nearby construction site.

As they drove up the long sloping rough stone approach road towards the site they passed an old stone building on their left with a two-metre high dry-stone wall around it. There were many children playing in front of it and in the road, who started to wave at them, then run alongside the van, Bob returned their waves. "What's this Hamid, a school?"

"No, it's what you call, hmm, how you say, home."

"Home?"

"Yes, they have, hmm, no family."

"It's an orphanage." Hamid agreed not really knowing what he had nodded his agreement to. "Stop Hamid."

"No Mr Bob, they will think you have got things for them, it's not good to stop."

"Hamid, stop NOW!" The van came to an abrupt halt. Just in front of them was a young dark olive skinned, long black-haired girl about five or six years old, in a dirty looking dark blue dress leant on the wall, with what looked like extremely poor condition and repaired many times pair of wooden crutches. She was waving and smiling at them. "I am getting out, Hamid."

"This is not good Mr Bob." Regardless of the warning Bob was out of the van and walking towards the girl with the other children now surrounding him. "Hello," said Bob as he arrived at the girl, "what's your name?"

"It's Fabi," came the answer from a small female teacher in her mid-thirties with short dark hair who had appeared from nowhere to stand alongside Bob. At this point of time she shouted at the other children in French, "aller a l'interieur," meaning "go inside" they followed her instruction and ran into the front of the building. "She can't talk English, but she does talk both Arabic and French very well. I am Anya," the teacher held her hand out to Bob, who shook hands with her.

"I am Bob from," before he could finish his sentence Anya said.

"I know where you are from," she pointed up the hill, "you are making that place, for them!"

"Come Mr Bob, we must go," said Hamid from behind him.

"Go now," said the teacher.

"No," came the reply, "I want to know about Fabi, her crutches are falling apart."

"Oh, we try to repair them, but it is, big problem."

Bob took his tape measure from where he always kept it on his trousers belt, then took a notepad and pencil out of the breast pocket of his checked shirt, knelt down and started to measure the crutches as he said, "can she not walk at all without them?"

"No, her legs do not work, she has, how you say, Polo?"

"Do you mean Polio?"

"That's it, it was two, no more than three years ago, we found her on the doorstep one morning." Anya ran her hand down a still smiling Fabi's hair, "she is good girl, no problem, good in class," she held her arms out, "her legs just no work. People come here to get children, but no one wants Fabi because of her legs, she would be, how you say, hmm, a big problem.

"Oh, that is so sad, Hamid," said Bob to his driver who was beside him.

"I know, we must go now, it is time to get food Mr Bob." Anya motioned to Fabi with her hand to return inside, she smiled at Bob and waved with her right hand which was returned, as she was led away.

"Hamid, that is really sad."

"Yes Mr Bob, very, very sad, we must go now!"

*

Over the next few days Bob got clothes off some of the workers for Peter. He took extra food when no one was in the canteen to pass to some of the other prisoners and guards who were now starting to turn a blind eye to him, particularly after he passed them a pack of cigarettes each and one day a bottle of beer, after Hamid had helped him change some Sterling for local currency at twenty-five to one on the black-market.

He and Hamid took some warm water one day so that Peter could have a shave and Bob cut his hair, very poorly by his own admission, and it didn't make things any better when he joked to Peter, "I am more used to cutting wood than I am hair!"

"Yes, I can see that," came the reply as he peered into the hand-held mirror.

Bob and Hamid had just pulled up outside the canteen to pick up the lunch time food when Colin came out of the offices and crossed the compound and called out. "Hi Bob, can you come into the office, Hugh Cameron the project manager wants a word."

"Oh, okay, I'll be back in a minute Hamid." Bob then followed Colin into the offices and was led down a corridor to the meeting room at the far end of the units where four tables made up a square, where a well-built Glaswegian in his mid-forties with thick curly black hair and clean-shaven face sat at the opposite side.

"Hello," said the newcomer as he leant across the tables to shake hands, "I am Bob." Before he could give his surname and without shaking hands the project manager said.

"I know who you are, sit down," he pointed to a chair, "and listen. I have been told by the chefs that since you have been taking the thief food up to the prison, that a lot more food has been disappearing. You take food to feed him and keep him alive, we are not feeding the whole fucking prison, the man is a thief do you understand?"

"Hugh, I have just been."

"DO YOU UNDERSTAND? And before you answer that question let me remind you, that you have only been here five-minutes and you are on a three-month probation, you can be sent home at any time." Bob sat and listened and it did pass through his mind to tell him to poke his job, then he remembered that Bob English prior to meeting Sam Crisp would have done just that. But no, he told himself to stay calm at all costs. "I've been out here a very long-time lad, these people will all take the piss if you let them, they will take the laces out of your boots and you will not know until they come off your fucking feet. Now do I make myself clear," he thumped the table with his right fist, "do you UNDERSTAND?"

Bob nodded his agreement and started to get up and as he did so he asked, "is that it?"

"Yes, you can go."

Bob turned and the left the office passing Colin who was stood in the doorway and walked along the corridor and mouthed to himself, "what a fucking wanker!"

*

"This is a good one Mr Bob, one of my cousins owns it, tell him you are my friend." Hamid pointed as he pulled the van over outside a small shop amongst a few houses one Friday morning. Friday was the holy day, and as she was having the day off and had not been away from the base camp, Bob had brought Sam with him saying.

"I want you to meet someone," but would not give her any more information than that. So, she had much intrigue when Bob returned from the shop about five minutes later and placed a large carrier bag in the rear of the van before returning to the front with her and Hamid.

"Bob what in hell's name is going on? You sneaked out to the canteen first thing this morning at the base camp, you're going in and out of shops, there's this mystery person I am going to meet, it's like James bloody Bond."

"Ok," came the reply, "this is what will happen, we will drop you at the Barna site, and we will go to the prison while you inspect the site, when we come back all will be revealed, okay?"

"Okay, but it had better be good with all this mucking around."

"I promise," smiled her boyfriend, "I promise, you will like it."

*

Bob and Hamid had to wait a short time for Sam when they returned from delivering Peters food. Bob had got extra food out of the base camp's canteen that morning to give to the other prisoners and guards as he did not want to up-set the chefs at Barna anymore.

When Sam came out of the office and got in the middle seat in the front of the van with the two males she said, "what an ignorant idiot that man is!"

"I take it you have just met Hugh Cameron?" Smiled Bob.

"Oh, you can't believe what I have been through with that man."

"Oh, I can, believe me I can."

"Well he has got his list, and I will be back in a few days, he can be sure of that!"

"I know you will."

"Right Mr English, let's forget him for now, where are we going, with this big mystery, oh it wasn't him you wanted me to meet, was it?"

"Nooo," he said as they drove down the slope from the site, "we are in fact," he pointed to his right, "we are in fact here." The van pulled up outside their destination.

"What's this?" Asked a now more than ever puzzled safety officer.

"It's an orphanage."

"Why are we going to an orphanage?"

"Right," he opened the door, "no more questions Miss Crisp, all will be revealed, very soon." He got out then said, "Hamid, you okay Hamid?"

"Yes Mr Bob, many okays." Bob and Sam made their way through the small front garden that was covered with weeds each side of a narrow footpath to a large wooden front door which had dark red paint peeling from it. Bob knocked on the horseshoe knocker which was fixed in the centre of the door, after a short time Anya opened the door.

"Oh, Mr Bob, welcome, come in, please, please."

"This is Sam," the two females shook hands, "my, aha, workmate, hmm co-worker," Bob stumbled with his words as his girlfriend smiled. "I would like Sam to meet Fabi, if that's ok?"

"Of course, Mr Bob, Miss Sam, come please, she is in the back-dining room at the moment." They were led through a large dirty white walled hallway, which had a staircase running up the right-hand wall, they then entered a large room at the rear of the property which had a very large white table in the centre with many chairs around it for the children to eat at.

Fabi was the only child in there as the rest were playing in the rear garden, she was sat on a small chair reading a book next to the large glass double doors, with her crutches on the floor beside her which appeared to be broken. When she saw Bob, a big smile came on her face and she waved to him which he returned as they rounded the table towards her.

"Sam, this is Fabi, she can't walk without her crutches, she's had Polio, she speaks French and Arabic, but no English."

"Her crutches have both broken over the last few days and our, how you say? Aha, odd-job-man is not here until next week, I have tried to fix them, but cannot. She has to crawl or be carried everywhere now." Anya reported.

"Oh," said Sam as she knelt beside her and held her hand, "Bonjour Fabi."

"Salut," replied the smiling child in French.

"Oh, can't we help her Bob?"

"Oh what, snap my fingers in the air and magic up a pair of crutches for a child, just like that?"

"Oh, Bob English don't be silly, you know what I mean?" Came the Snapped reply, with a hint of annoyance.

"Oh, do I know now?" He turned to see Hamid's head appear around the door, Bob then snapped the fingers of his right hand in the air twice and said, "Hamid please enter." Without replying the driver entered the room with both hands behind his back. When he reached Bob, he brought them both around to his front to show in the left the bag of sweets Bob had purchased that morning and, in the right, he had a parcel wrapped in brown paper with some blue rope tied around it like a bow, the shape looked very much like a pair of child's crutches. The three females all

129

squealed at once as Bob took the parcel and passed it to Sam. "Please, would you do the honours Miss Crisp," Sam took the package, then without any more a-to-do the two females on the floor ripped at the packaging to expose a new pair of crutches that Bob had made in the sites workshop over the past few days with the help of the workshop's joiner.

They had planned down timber and used bolts from the site, Hamid had taken Bob to a local rubbish dump and they purchased an old leather armchair, for padding under the arms and the leather to cover the padding.

As quick as a flash as if she had no problem at all, Fabi was on her feet with the crutches under her arms and made it across the room to Bob who dropped to his knees to hug the approaching child.

"You bugger Bob," Sam joined them and thumped him on the arm, "you've made me cry," she wiped her eyes.

"And me," said Anya.

"And me," said Hamid.

"Oh, bloody hell I am with a load of softies." He stood up and took the bag of sweets and held them open for Fabi to have first pick then handed them to Anya and said, "these are for the other children, you do it, I don't want to get mobbed." She took the bag as Sam took Fabi back to her chair and started to talk to her in French. Bob then asked Anya, "where's the toilet please, I need to go?"

"Out there," she pointed to the woods past where the children were playing on the rough ground.

"Oh, right, where, I can't see them?"

"It's the woods, Mr Bob," said Hamid from behind him.

"You're joking, this is a wind up?"

"No Mr Bob, that's where we go," reported Anya, "all of us and the children, we have no toilets." Bob seemed speechless, then said.

"We will talk in a minute," then made off towards the woods. When he was finished he spent some time walking around the playground and talking to Hamid who had joined him along with Anya, as the children greedily ate their sweets. Anya shouted to the children.

"Ramasse le papier," in French, "pick up the paper."

Sam and Fabi were deep in conversation when the others returned to them. "Okay, we have got to go, I have got to get Peter's lunch up to the prison."

"Ok, Fabi," Sam nodded to her, as the young child said in English as the safety officer mouthed to her.

"Thank you, Mr Bob, you are very kind." Bob wiped his eyes then dropped to his knees as the three hugged together.

The three workers were back in the van before they started talking again, after a very tearful goodbye.

"What a lovely little girl, and you never told me, you bugger," she thumped Bob on the arm again.

"I wanted it to be a surprise."

"Well it was that, but such a nice one, thank you Bob," she kissed him on the cheek. "Fabi was full of questions."

"Such as?"

"She wanted to know if we were married?"

"Oh."

"I said not yet," the female smiled at this, then said, "she asked had we come to take her home with us?"

"Oh no, no one wants her because of her legs."

"I know, she told me, she said they don't work, people want children whose legs work."

"What did you say about us taking her home?"

"I said we can't, but we will visit her as much as we can while we are here. She told me they think her mother is local and her father Iranian, he came here as a worker. She was about two when they left her on the doorstep. I asked her when her birthday is, and she said she does not have one."

"Oh God, it's so sad, and she is lovely. I also want to do something about the toilets there, or should I say the lack of them."

"That wouldn't be easy, would it, there's no drainage?" Asked Sam.

"There is a way with no drains, Hamid has explained it to me, they use them a lot in Africa, they are called 'long-drops.' I think we could sort it out, but I would have to ask that idiot Cameron, and I really don't think he will help them."

"Well if it's any help, the general foreman Kevin Archer said to me, that if the list wasn't done soon he would get it done next week as Cameron goes home for two weeks this coming Tuesday."

"Well now, that's interesting," Bob thought for a few moments, "I think that Kevin is okay, I have had a few chats with him. The thing is we wouldn't have long, and it's not a five-minute job you know. And of course, I would have to get Kevin on side first."

"Take him down there when Cameron has gone on leave, get him to see it all, we can get him to meet Fabi, if that doesn't pull at his heart strings nothing will."

"Okay, you know, no doubt I will get sacked, but guess what? I don't care, let's do it." Sam held his hand, then kissed him on the cheek and said.

"You go, I go!"

*

It was a lot easier than Bob thought to get Kevin to agree, he did take him down to the orphanage and he said "yes." But said they could not let Colin know as he told Hugh everything, so they would have to be careful how they got the materials etc down there. Kevin said Colin was like clockwork regarding the times he went to eat so they agreed as soon as he went to the canteen they would be ready to make their moves.

It wasn't a five-minute job, but it was done a lot faster then Bob had first thought, in fact it was done in just over a week. Kevin and Bob marked it all out and agreed how to build it. The ground was very hard which while it was not easy to dig, with the mini-digger they took down, there was little chance of the sides caving in. The whole pit was ten-foot deep by five-foot wide by twenty-foot long. They formed a plywood shutter decking with four small boxings in them for each of the cubicles for the human waste to go down. Stood behind these, long vent pipes were placed in the air to vent the waste smell above the roof. This was then concreted with steel mesh reinforcement in it.

When that was complete, ten in number, ten-foot long wooden posts were concreted in the ground standing up straight, three levels of four by two-inch timbers were fixed to the posts on two sides and the rear, to which red metal roof cladding was fixed, to form the roof. At the front four wooden frames, plywood doors were fitted. When all of this was complete one of the site painters was brought down to decorate the four doors and put signs saying, Garcons, Les filles, Hommes, Dames, translated from French to English meaning, boys, girls, men and ladies.

The lads who had worked on it all clubbed together to buy the first large supply of the chemicals that was needed to rot the waste and limit the smell.

It was on the Friday before Hugh Cameron came back that Bob, Sam, Hamid, Kevin and other workers gathered for the grand opening. Some blue rope was tied across the front of the new toilet block and to great cheers Bob cut the rope with a pair of blue bolt croppers, usually used for cutting steel mesh and announced in a loud voice in the French Sam had taught him and he had written on some paper, "les toilettes prêtes à l'emploi. The toilets are ready to use!"

*

"What do you mean he wants us to pick him up?" Asked Bob in a very surprised tone as he and Sam sat in the canteen at the base camp eating their evening meal the Monday night before the day that Hugh Cameron was due back. They had been joined by the office manager Dave who had told them that Hugh had rang James Hardwick from home and said he wanted Sam and Bob to pick him up at the airport the following evening.

"That's what I have been told to tell you by James, the flight should be in at seven pm, bring him back here, he has a meeting first thing on Wednesday, then he is going back to his site at Barna." The manager turned and left the two staring at each other, only to be broken by Bob who said.

"He knows!"

"I think so," came the reply.

"Well fuck him, sorry Sam, he can get us sacked, and fuck him again, and sorry again Sam."

"If we were going to get sacked, they would do it here, surely?"

"Yes, your right, again Miss Crisp, maybe he's going to murder us and dump our bodies in a dich?" They both laughed at this then Sam replied.

"I wouldn't put it past the mad sod. I'll tell you what, let's make the most of it, you sort Hamid out to get the evening food up to Peter and we will bugger off into Algiers for the afternoon, before we get murdered that is!"

*

The two co-workers did bunk off work after lunch time the next day and spent the afternoon having some down time in the capital city. They walked around the 'old town' and in and out of shops. Sam purchased two long dresses and headscarves like the local women wore. Bob declined to buy the Fez hat and cloak that was put on him from behind by the shopkeeper without giving permission as he waited for his girlfriend to try the garments on. After the shopping was complete they sat outside a Café in the afternoon sunshine drinking coffee and eating, Kouigan-amann, sweet dough cakes with butter.

As Hamid had Bob's van the two used one of the minibuses to collect the project manager. The two also agreed that it would be a good opportunity for Bob to drive out there, getting used to the opposite side of the road.

"There he is," said Bob as they waited for Cameron by the airport's arrival area. "God, he looks as pissed as a fart." They watched a very intoxicated looking and swaying Hugh Cameron make his way towards them. Very little was said as Bob carried his suitcase to the mini bus. Bob got back in the driver's seat and Sam sat on the double seat beside him as the project manager sat on the row of seats behind the two, but instead of sitting back he leaned forward to talk to them as Bob drove off.

"Take that way over there," he pointed into the dark night.

"Oh, it's okay, I know the way thanks Hugh," the driver replied.

"For fuck sake," he barked for those in the front to get a full blast of the Scotch Whisky he had been consuming. "Do as you are fucking told for once, now go that way, I've been working here over twenty fucking years, you have only been here five fucking minutes." Bob did no more than what he was told.

The driver put the head lights on full beam as they travelled along the unlit and very dark road with no other vehicles in sight when the voice from behind them said. "I know what you have done, Colin phoned me at home, I will have you both fucking sacked for this, try to make a fool of me will you? Well I'll tell you no one does that to me. Giving these fucking locals our fucking gear to build fucking toilets, they are used to shitting in the woods, let them carry on doing that, I say. Take that road up there," he pointed, the driver duly did as he was told. "I've been in this game longer than you two have been out of fucking nappies!"

The mini bus drove up the sloping approach to join a major well-lit highway, it was when they saw the headlights in the distance coming towards them and vehicles on the opposite side of the carriageway beyond a low barrier going in their direction that Sam shouted.

"SHIT, we are going the wrong way up a motorway!"

"Fuck," said the driver, as he spun the mini bus around, at one point almost turning it over. From behind them was a loud bang as Hugh flew sideways and hit his head on the side window, then crashed to the floor. Bob managed to get the mini bus off at the slip road they had come the wrong way up. When it was safe to do so Bob pulled over. After a few moments of silence, the driver said, "can you fucking believe that, we nearly got killed."

"Bloody hell," came the reply from Sam. Without turning around Bob said.

"You took us the wrong way up a fucking motorway Hugh." They sat and waited for the shouted, smelly reply, but there was none. The two looked at each other then turned and looked over the seat at an unconscious project manager laying behind their seat on the floor.

"Hugh?" Asked Sam, "hello Hugh." They both looked at each other again.

"Is he dead?" Asked the driver.

"You're the first aider," replied the passenger.

"Well if he needs the kiss of life, he's had it, no chance, he can piss off." It was at that point the body on the floor made some noises and moved slightly.

"He's alive, let's get him back to the camp," said Sam, they drove back to the base camp and got the medic who told them.

"Let him sleep it off." They then got security to help him to the room he had been allocated for the night.

The two were just finishing breakfast the next morning in a packed canteen when Cameron came in and stood at the end of their table and said with a very visible lump on his forehead.

"I am not finished with you two, there is no way you are going to get away with what you did while I was on leave. I will have you both on the next flight out of here, we are not here to look after fucking locals." The two were not sure if the smell of whiskey was from the night before or a fresh intake that morning!

Sam wiped her mouth and said in a calm voice. "That is your prerogative Mr Cameron, and you shall be on a flight home shortly after that." She took a breath, "because as soon as I return to the UK, I will contact the head office and see the MD, Colin Johnston, whom I happen to have known very well for many years, and I tell him that you flew on an airline that we are all told that we must not drink before boarding. You were so drunk you could not walk in a straight line, and that you made us go the wrong way up a motorway, and nearly caused a massive road traffic accident and get us all killed because of your drinking. Also, that you shouted and told a local family at the airport to fuck 'off!'" At this point all workers in the canteen was listening to Sam. "Or Hugh, you can take the glory of helping a local orphanage that had no toilets and had to use the woods." The whole canteen was waiting for the reply which never came, as the project manager turned and slammed the door as he exited the canteen to great cheers from the workforce.

"He didn't swear at a local family Sam."

"Yeah, little lie, but he was so pissed he doesn't know what he did, and also I don't know the MD, and I used the name Colin Johnston, who's an old friend of mine, but he doesn't know that either," smiled the safety officer.

Chapter 11

Free at Last.

"Next week?"

"Yes, next Wednesday." Bob was sitting in the cell with Peter and had just told him about his court date. "I have got to pick you up from here on Wednesday evening, take you back to the camp, you are spending the night there, they want you cleaned up as it seems the press is going to be there."

"What do you think I will get Bob?"

"Oh, it's all been settled apparently, all agreed, I know what you're getting, they are going to give you three months in prison."

"Oh, shit Bob, I can't last another three months here, I have already done three."

"Oh, sorry Peter, did I not say, deemed served, you will be out of the country on Friday," the storyteller smiled

"You wanker."

"Well, what is life for if a person can't have a bit of fun every now and then?"

"Oh," sighed the prisoner from the side of his bed as he drew on a cigarette that Bob had brought in for him. "I can't wait, this has been the longest three months of my life, I know I did wrong, but believe me I have been punished spending twelve weeks in here," he looked around the cell."

"Well, it's almost over Peter."

"Thanks Bob," he hugged his new friend.

On the morning of the court case Bob picked Peter from the Barna camp for the ten-o'clock hearing, the accused was dressed in new clothes that the company had provided. As they left the compound in the van Bob saw Hugh Cameron outside of the office talking to the company's official photographer, the project manager glared at Bob as they passed.

They then had five minutes at the orphanage to drop off some sweets Sam had brought and given to Bob and to say hello to Fabi.

The hearing was the first case on, Peter had an interrupter who pleaded, "coupable," guilty in French for him. It was as Bob said, three months deemed served, and immediate deportation.Bob saw him off at the airport the next day, Peter was looking very bleary eyed after spending the previous night until kicking out time in the camps bar.

*

"Have you seen this in the news sheet that Kingston & Easton put out each month?" Asked Sam, as she held the single sheet of A3 paper for Bob to see, as they sat down for their evening meal a few weeks after the incident with Hugh Cameron regarding them having the long drop built at the orphanage.

Bob read the banner headline, which said, "Baran project builds toilets for children."And beneath that was a photograph of Hugh, Kevin, Colin, Anya and some children including Fabi on her new crutches in front of the toilet block and Hugh going on to comment.

"I found out how much the children and staff of the orphanage needed this facility, so I felt it was the least, we on site, and on behalf of Kingston & Easton, could do to help the people who have been so kind to us in this country."

"What a fucking tosser," spat Bob, "sorry Sam. I mean can you believe he has done that?"

"Yes, I can, he could have had us sacked, but then he would have had to explain why he sacked us, and that was because we helped some local children. He's just saving face Bob." Sam replied.

"Saving face, he's a two faced tosser, that's what he is," snapped Bob with his anger showing.

"Bob," she held his hand across the table, "we know it was you, the orphanage and the lads know. Look, people like Hugh have to come out on top, the truth is, we knew he wouldn't take it lying down, if he couldn't get rid of us. He's won this time, but as you once told me, every dog has his day."

"Bow wow," Bob smiled at her, then after a few seconds of thinking time he continued. "And the thing is there is only one person to point the finger at," he pointed across the table at Sam, "you!"

"WHY?" Came the loud snapped surprised reply.

"Cast your mind back Miss Crisp, you told Hugh, in this canteen," he pointed at the table, "that he could sack us, or take the glory of building the toilets himself."

"Oh, bloody hell," she hit herself on her forehead with the palm of her left hand, then said, "guess what?"

"What?"

"The mans a fucking tosser!"

*

"Dead?" Asked Sam.

"Seems like it," replied James Hardwick, whose jet-black hair seemed to be running onto his forehead.

"What happened?" asked Bob as they sat in the manager's office.

"I know very little about it, I have just been told to get you two over there as soon as possible, it is a long journey, you can stay at one of the other camps overnight on the way, it will take about two days to drive there.

"Well then, we had better get going," said Sam as they all stood up. "Let's pop and see Fabi," said Sam as the two got in the van, we may not see her for a little while and I've got the French to English book for her in the room, I'll go and get it."

"Yes, well, I could do with going into the city, I promised one of the lads I would sort some paperwork out for him at our embassy."

"Paperwork, that's for the office to sort out, surely?"

"Oh, it's complicated, I said I would do it, to help out. Look drop me off, pop and see Fabi with the book, then come back for me and we will be on our way."

"Okay, let's go."

It did in fact take over two days to drive down to the site at Tamra, which was south of the base camp. Sam and Bob had both changed English money up through Hamid before they had started their journey south, not knowing how long they would be away.

They had been given maps etc of how to get to Tamra and had taken it in turns to drive. Many of the roads were straight and with little new to see, it would have been easy to lose concentration and possibly fall asleep, so they talked to each other and at times sang together and played 'I Spy' as they drove. "Something beginning with 'S' for sand" was banned.

They could see the camp as they approached. The different size camps that were being built across the country depended on what forces would be stationed there, a battalion, company, brigade, regiment etc.

This camp was large for a battalion, the same as Barna and would house about three-hundred personnel. These camps were made up of rows of double storey barrack blocks, officer quarters and some for married ones, large canteen areas, library's, gyms, sport fields and weapon stores. All of the buildings and surrounding high walls were made of large precast concrete units that were made in moulds and shutters on site. The units where fixed to an upright steel girder frame.

Whilst there was still a lot of work to do within the camp area a lot of the external fifteen-foot high wall panels had been completed for security reasons, and some of the high look-out-towers were also in place, it gave the appearance of an old wild west fort from the USA as they approached.

"What happened then?" Asked the female safety officer as she and Bob talked to Ian Carter, a very large, bushy ginger haired man with the same wild looking beard from the north of Scotland. Ian was the foreman over the precast concrete gang and also the gang that fitted the units. It was one of his men that had been killed when a one-and-a-half-ton unit had fallen on him as they were erecting them up straight to form the external walls of a barrack block.

"Well thing is lass, I wasn't there at the time," Ian reported in a thick Scottish accent, as the three stood in the precast yard. While it was partially cloudy the fact they had moved a lot further south towards the Sahara Desert and the equator, even with it being near the end of the year it was very hot. Sam had removed the scarf from her head as she mainly did when on site."But I did find out what happened and have made a report out."

"Yes, I do have a copy, thank you," replied the safety officer as she continued taking notes.

"The thing is," the Scotsman continued, "Davy wasn't dead when they left here in the ambulance that the medic drove up here in. He, Joe the medic was totally pissed, arseholed."

"Nooo," said Bob.

"Yes. We all ran over there when we heard what happened and got the unit off him. When Joe got here you could smell the drink on him."

"Could it have been from the night before?" Asked Sam.

"No Sam lass, everyone knows he drinks all the time, I sent one of my lads to be in the back of the ambulance with Davy going to the hospital, he said they nearly crashed many times and Davy almost came off the bed a few times."

"If everyone knows the medic is drinking all the time, how come he is still here, and hasn't been sacked?" Asked Bob.

"They can't get the medical staff, that's what I have been told," Ian continued.

"Okay," continued Sam, "I will look into that. I want to go through the method procedure you use for fixing the units, and see if there is any way we can improve it. And I will be doing a safety list for the whole site and I will start with this compound, it needs a really good tidy and clean up."

"We are very busy lass, and I am losing two men next week as they go home for Christmas."

"We are both here for Christmas and New Year," moaned Bob, "third bloody Christmas in a row I have been away from my girls."

"I am home for New Year, Hogmanay," continued Ian.

"Oh," continued Bob, "we are not home until the end of Jan."

"Well," replied Ian, but before he could say anymore Sam, keen to keep on the subject interrupted with.

"Yes, look Bob, why don't you go and meet some of the lads and see if there is anything you need to sort there and I will sort things out with Ian, then have a walk around site." Before he could reply, she continued as she looked at her wrist watch, "let's meet in the canteen at one, for lunch?"

"Okay, I will do as I am told Miss Crisp," he saluted with his right hand and stood to attention. This was greeted by a push in his chest.

They both spent the next two hours at their respective duties. Bob was starting to hear more about Joe the Medic as he talked to the lads, but felt it best not to approach him until he had spoken to Sam, then maybe have a word with the project manager together.

It was a little after one o'clock when Sam joined Bob who was sitting at a six-seater table at the back of the large canteen packed with workers with Ian and some of his co-workers. Sam sat next to Bob with a tray containing her lunch. As she sat there was a click above them on the rear wall at the 'fly trap' a blue electric ring.

"Six," commented Ian.

"Six what?" Asked Bob.

"Six dead flies' so far today, me and the lads have a bet each day, how many dead fly's there are at all the meal breaks during the day, the person furthest from the final total has to get the first round of beer in that night.

"Oh," came the puzzled reply from Bob. "Oh, by the way Sam, I have put us both down for twenty-five pound each for the collection for Davy, the lad who died, for his family they will take it out of next months wages.

"That's fine, well done. Do you know what?" The female asked Bob, "when I was at the counter getting served, a chap walked in who is a real look-a-like for the brother of the drain layer who got his fingers cut off in the Falklands."

"Oh, what was his name?" Came the reply.

"Was it Joe?" Asked the safety officer.

"Joe Johnson, and his brother who had the accident was Kevin, Yorkshiremen."

"We have got two drain laying brothers here," put in Ian, "they are in fact Joe and Kevin from Yorkshire, but their surname is not Johnson, it's, hmm, Simpson, and one of them wears a glove on his right hand all the time, no matter how hot it gets, says it is to protect an old injury." Sam and Bob looked at each other, then the safety officer asked her boyfriend.

"Are you thinking what I am thinking?"

"I am."

"What's that?" Asked Ian.

"No nothing, just a coincidence, come on Bob, let's eat up, I've got a lot to do yet, and I could do with a hand."

*

"That's them okay," said Bob as he and Sam looked at the brother's passports in the site office with office manager Daniel Herbert the tall well-built 53-year-old from Brighton in Sussex and project manager Ken Danby, a 46-year-old, small in height, round-faced bald-headed man from Bedfordshire.

"Are you sure?" Asked Ken.

"Oh, yes," said Sam, "that is definitely them, but they went under the name of Johnson in the Falklands."

"Well," put in Daniel, "the passports look real."

"Maybe they are, and they went to the Falklands on fake one's. The rumour was that Kevin had his fingers cut off before they went out there. And that he got paid compensation from the other company and was going to claim from JLB as well. It was just before a ship came in, they sent him home 'Air Bridge' then his brother jacked and went on that ship, I wonder if they are going to try and do the same here?" Asked Bob.

"Well," said Ken, "Kevin does keep the glove on all the time, and I wouldn't like to lose them, but there's no fucking way they are going to pull that stroke on my fucking site. Come on you two, let's go down and fucking have it out with them, I won't be beating about the fucking bush." The two visitors looked at each other as Ken marched off.

The three went in the project managers Range Rover some distance to the far end of the site where the brothers were laying six-inch clay pipes with a JCB digger in front of them digging the trench.

The Rover pulled up in front of the machine and the three got out and approached the two workers. "Hello, Joe, Kevin, fancy seeing you lads here?" Said Bob.

The two stopped and looked up, and showed surprised to see them. They looked at each other and before they could answer Ken said.

"I will start by saying," he held one finger up in front of him, "I haven't got time to fuck about. These two said you were in the Falklands under a different name, aha?"

"Johnson," put in Sam. Joe went to talk.

"Shut," Ken pointed at them, "the fuck up, I am talking. Right, where was I? Yes, they say you," he pointed at Kevin, "had your fingers cut off, but everyone reckoned it was a scam to get fucking compo, right?" He pointed at Kevin again, "take that fucking glove off, now!"

"It's an old hand injury."

"Then there is no fucking problem taking the fucking glove off THEN!" Snarled Ken.

"Why should he?" Asked Joe.

"Because this is my fucking site, and if he doesn't take the fucking glove off NOW, as your both still on fucking probation, you'll both be on the next fucking plane home, your fucking choice!" Joe nodded to his brother who then removed the glove to expose a fingerless right hand. "Hold both fucking hands in the air at head height," barked the manager. He then took a small camera out of his trousers pocket and took two photographs. "Right it's confirmed, no fucking fingers there, and in front of two wittiness, I'll be keeping my fucking eye on you two from now on. Come on you two, let's go."

When Sam and Bob got out of the Range Rover at the office and were on their own, Bob reported, "I am glad Ken took that well, bloody hell you wouldn't want to get on the wrong side of him when he doesn't take it well!"

*

The pair finished their work at Tamra after a couple of days, reports were made out, and a long safety list made up by Sam, and put in place a safe method to fix the large concrete panels. Sam said she would now, "implement this method across all the sites in the country."

Some of the lads did talk to Bob about Ken the project manager, about his attitude towards the workforce, not paying the correct overtime hours some of the lads had worked and his, "if you don't like it get the next fucking plane out of here, and there's plenty on the dole at home, we'll get them out here."

As Bob attended a meeting with the project manager on the morning of the day they were to leave site, which he wasn't looking forward to it very much. He had said to Sam, "I've made the meeting the last thing I do before we leave site, then if Ken goes mad and tries to murder me, you can have the van running and I'll just jump in and we can do a runner." He laughed

As it happened things did not go too bad in the meeting. Regarding the overtime payments he said it was his, "general foreman Jon Fulton who deals with that, I will get it sorted." He did in fact agree with Bob regarding the way he talks to lads at times and said, "I know I should calm down, but the fuckers just wind me up at times, and I lose it! I have been told by the medic my blood pressure is through the roof at times."

As the medic had been brought up Bob mentioned about his drinking, Ken replied. "I know, and I have given the fucker his final warning and told him he will be on the plane the next time he drinks in the day again."

"You must have a medic on site at all times Ken, you can't not have one," put in Bob.

"I told him, you told me that an extra medic had just arrived at the base camp from the UK and they are looking for a posting for him," replied the project manager with a smile."

"I did?" Asked a surprised Bob.

"No, you didn't, but that fat fucker doesn't know that!"

*

When Sam and Bob had left Tamra for the base camp they had two other smaller sites on the return journey to visit, the first being Ratner and the second was outside a small-town called Moura. They reached Ratner by early afternoon, and after their inspections and talks with the manager they spent the night there, then headed off the next morning after breakfast as it was a long drive to Moura, and again they would be spending the night at the site.

As they got nearer the roads were wet as it had been raining since the night before. As they got near the site Sam, who was the passenger at this point, put her head scarf on. As they approached the town they could see the site at the end of the road, about a hundred metres away, but a market had been set up on each side of the road as it was normally held on the open field in front of the site, but because of the rain that area was too wet to use.

Very slowly Bob made his way along the road as there were people walking around them and cars coming from the opposite direction there was not much room to make any mistakes. As the white van with the companies name on each side was just over half way along the road a group of three men stood in front of the vehicle, causing Bob to stop abruptly. The three started banging on the bonnet and were shouting at them. "Bob, make sure your door is locked, they don't look very happy!" Within a short space of time other men joined the three, at each side of the vehicle and started rocking it from side to side. "Shit," said Sam, "don't go too fast, but I think you had better start inching along to get us out of here." The driver did as he was instructed without saying a word in reply. They continued doing this until they got to the end of the market road and to the access road across the field, the would-be hijackers who had continued banging as they walked backwards then dispersed.

They continued into the site without a word then pulled up in the small car parking area in front of a small site office, inside the walled compound.

"Bloody hell," said Bob while sitting in the van for a few moments after stopping, "what in God's name was that all about?"

"I thought we were going to get murdered, come here, I need a hug." The two embraced each other for a short while until a knock on the window drove them apart. Outside was Jimmy Andrews the general foreman who ran the site, the small sites were run by a general foreman only. He was a short stocky mid forty's fair-haired man from Stoke-on-Trent. Bob wound his window down.

"Don't let me break anything up," he smiled. Bob told him what had just happened. "Oh, they get a bit like that at times here."

"Blimey, we have never come across anything like that before." Bob replied.

"Well, I suppose sacking three of them this morning for nicking didn't help."

"That will do it," put in Sam.

"Oh, don't worry about them, they were only trying to frighten you."

"Well they bloody done that okay," snapped Bob.

"Oh, come on, I'll show you around the site." The two newcomers exchanged looks before getting out to join Jimmy.

The small sites were just a smaller model of the large ones, but all the precast units came in from the base camp. After Sam had made her list they returned to the office for a meeting regarding safety, when it was finished Jimmy said. "Come on, I will buy you a beer," he looked at his wrist watch, "the bar has just opened."

They walked along a walk-way for about twenty metres between offices on the right-hand side and port-a-cabins accommodation on the left, all in white with the canteen and bar at the end. By entering at a centre door, the bar area was to the right, in the middle were tables and chairs and at the far-left-hand end of the sixty by twenty-five-foot unit was the kitchen and serving hatch. The two took in the view. Red and white bunting tape, otherwise used to fence off dangerous work areas run around the walls and across the canteen as Christmas decorations. At the far end of the bar was what looked like a Christmas tree, at eight-foot-high it almost touched the ceiling. Running in circles around the tree was blue draw rope. Hanging off many branches by the pull caps were beer cans that were covered in silver tin foil that had been acquired from the kitchen, on the top of the tree was a large star again covered with foil.

"Wow," said Sam, "I love it, the whole place looks great, where did you get the tree from, they don't do Christmas here?"

"Here, I'll show you," the three walked to the door and Jimmy pointed beyond the compound to a row of very tall conifer trees that run along the east side of the site, they were all the same height apart from one which was eight foot shorter than the others. "We put one of the lads up there on a pallet on the forklift, he cut it off with a bow saw."

"I didn't hear that," smiled the safety officer.

"Oh, I forgot who I was talking to, all done safely of cause. Come on, I'll buy you that beer." The three went back to the bar/canteen which now had workers queueing for food.

"What's that all about," asked Bob, pointing to a line of football pennants running across the top of the bar, some showing the teams name and some a blank side.

"It's the lads football teams, if the team loses they are turned around until they win again."

"If my team, Brentford was up there," moaned Bob, "it would be forever turned around!"

*

Two things woke the pair up the next morning in the twin bed port-a-cabin they had been given for the night. The first, at six-fifteen am, was the Friday call to prayers which was broadcast across the town by loud speakers, one of which was very close to the site. The other was the smell of bacon, an item that could not be purchased in the country.

"What's that?" Asked Sam as she woke in the bed facing Bob.

"Oh, it's Friday prayers," replied Bob, "you know that by now," as he turned over in the bed.

"No," came the reply, "that smell, coming through the air vent."

Bob rolled back over to take a sniff, "oh, its bacon," and then went to roll back, he then jumped up and shouted, "BACON!"

"Oh," came the reply from Sam as she joined Bob both in their nightwear in the middle of the room, "I can't remember the last time we had bacon."

"Nor can I, come on let's get dressed and get some before it all goes!" The pair made their way to the canteen after getting washed and dressed, there were a few workers already there. After a short while of eating a full breakfast of bacon, baked beans, sausage, fried eggs and fried bread and Heinz tomato ketchup and coffee which had also been purchased in the UK they were joined by Jimmy.

"Good morning," he greeted them, "how's the breakfast, this fine morning?" He smiled.

"This is the best meal I have had since, I can't remember when," said Bob between mouth falls, "where did you get the bacon from?"

"Every time one of the lads goes on leave I get them to bring things back, the bacon and sausages they go in the freezer and I get the money back on expenses for them."

"And you have never been questioned about it?" Asked the safety officer.

"The first time I did, but I said we are a small site and there is a food budget so take it out of that, I have never been questioned since. I got lads bringing loads of gear back for Christmas, I am going to pick up the turkeys next week."

"Where are you getting them from?" Asked Bob.

"The base camp. They have been breeding them all year, they have got loads, it is in fact," he whispered, "meant to be a surprise for the lads. Right, I have got to get on," he stood up and shook hands with both of them, "see you again," he turned and left.

"I," said Sam, she pointed to her chest, "have just had a brilliant idea."

"What?" Came the reply.

"Let's do Christmas dinner for the orphanage."

"They don't do Christmas here," said Bob after he took a sip of coffee.

"That's the whole point, surely. We get everything together, get the turkeys and whatever we need, and we can get the chefs at Barna to cook it in the morning, we know they are not having Christmas dinner until night time there."

"Sam, it's a loving idea, I would love to do it for the kids, but there is no way that ignorant bloody Hugh Cameron would agree to it, you know that. We, me and you," he pointed to himself and Sam, "are not on top of his like list," he took another sip of his drink, then continued, "in fact, he heats us."

"You say that, he got all the glory for the toilets, we can use that," she held his hand across the table, "oh come on Mr English, it would be great if we could pull it off."

"Yes, and it's a very big IF!"

"Oh, come on Bob," she lifted his hand and kissed it, "where's your sense of adventure? Please!"

"You know you get your way with me every time, don't you?"

"Yes," she smiled as she got up, "it's only just over a week away, we have got loads to do, come on, let's go"

Chapter 12

We call it Christmas.

"You have got to be joking!" Snapped Hugh across the desk in his office at Sam and Bob who sat in chairs opposite him after requesting to see him, Colin sat in a chair on Cameron's side of the desk. "I have told you two before," he pointed across the table, "we are not here to spend time and money on locals who can't look after themselves."

"It's an orphanage Hugh," put in Bob, "we just want to bring them a bit of joy at Christmas."

"Right, in case you have not noticed this is a Muslim country, they don't do CHRISTMAS HERE!!!"

"We just want to make the children happy for a few hours, it won't cost you anything if you don't want to contribute, we can source all the food etc, we need you to ask the chefs to do the food for us?" Bob pleaded.

"I am very busy," Hugh stood up. "I consider this meeting to be concluded." Sam, who had remained silent to that point, took the folded newsletter out of her inside jacket pocket and opened it up and pushed it across the desk with what Hugh had said regarding helping the orphanage highlighted in yellow.

"You mean to say," she said, "the person who went to all that trouble to build the children's toilets cannot help with Christmas dinner and some toys. Or shall we make it common knowledge that you were in fact going to have us two sacked over it?" Hugh sat down and looked at the paper on the desk and before he could reply the safety officer continued. "Or you can help us out and have more photos down there helping the children, and it's only going cost a few quid out of petty cash for a few gifts, and some wine and beer for the helpers." There was a tense silence for a few moments which was broken by Colin who said.

"It will help with the new stream managers position coming up for grabs Hugh. Good publicity!" Again, there was silence in the room with three people waiting for the project managers response. After a short while he stood up and said.

"Colin, you sort it with them, but you two," he pointed across the table, "are now taking the fucking piss, this is the last time, do you understand?" He left the office without waiting for an answer, slamming the door as he went. Again, there was silence which was broken by Bob who said.

"I am pleased we have his full backing," he smiled.

"I will warn you two, don't push him too far, I have known him a long time, just be careful, I know you mean well for the children, but be careful."

"Thank you, Colin," replied Sam as they both got to their feet, "we will."

"You two," continued the office manager, "need to get your residency papers sorted before you go on leave in January, for returning here after your leave, you can only be visitors for three months."

"Yes, we know," replied Bob. "We were going to get it sorted through the base camp, it's all in hand."

"Bring your passports up here in a day or so and I will sort it all for you. You both need a medical, ID, photos, a visit to the police station, I will get you a French interrupter for the day."

"We have both had medicals before we came out and ID photos and Sam speaks fluent French," replied Bob.

"It doesn't work like that up here Bob, let's say it's all agreed, we hmm, we pay the local authorities, and you get your visas to stay, it's all above board, but that's how it works. Doing it that way, let's say, smooths the way for us dealing with the locals here, do I make my point?"

"Fine," said Sam, "you sort it and we will be legal, we have got to go, there's loads to sort out before Christmas."The two left the offices together, once outside Bob said.

"We hadn't said anything about toys, beer and wine, you slipped them in!"

"In for a penny, in for a pound Mr English," smiled the female.

*

It was a very busy few days for the two leading up to the festivities, after leaving Colin they had gone to the orphanage,

Bob talked to Anya regarding Christmas dinner, telling her, "do not tell anyone, let's just make it a surprise," she agreed to this.

The morning they were to get their papers authorised they popped into the orphanage with sweets. Sam sat with Fabi and her French to English book which she was enjoying, using new words with Sam.

Before Bob and Sam left the orphanage to go to the town and their appointments for the residency, Sam and Fabi called Bob over to the chair Fabi was sat on in the dining room next to the glass doors, she put her arms out to Bob who went down on his knees, she hugged him and said.

"I love you Mr Bob, and you Miss Sam," the three hugged. The two adults were both wiping their eyes as they walked back to the van to continue their journey into town.

"She's lovely," said Sam as they got in the van, "and so clever, such a shame about her legs."

"You know we will have to say goodbye to her forever one day Sam," Bob observed as he started the van up.

"I know, and it is going to be so hard when that day comes."

"Yes, your right, but unfortunately that's life."

"I know, come on, let's get down the town and get this lot over with, before they chuck us in jail or something." The female smiled.

The first stop was to meet the interrupter, Hanna, a slim short dark-haired woman in her mid-thirties whom they had been given money from Colin for. She just happened to be the wife of one of the police officers. The next stop was for photographs, Hanna's English was very poor so Sam ended up doing most of the talking.

It was then on to the doctors, who in fact had very good English and been to England a few times. When he found out Bob came from London he seemed surprised that he did not know his friends who lived in Rose Street, Hackney.

The two laughed when they came out, discussing what had happened. They had their blood pressure taken, with two pumps on the pump they were both told their pressure was "very good." Then they were taken into an empty ten-foot by four-foot white painted cupboard with a single light bulb hanging from the ceiling and told they were having a chest x-ray. They had to strip to the waist, Sam refused to take her bra off.

"I wasn't going to have him looking and staring at me," she told Bob later. Then the doctor went outside, turned the light on and off twice, opened the door told them to turn around, and repeated the action, then told them both.

"You are both very fit," after Bob had handed more money over of course. It was then on to the police station with the photographs and letters from the doctor and the last of the money Colin had given them to get their passports stamped with a residence visa. As they were about to leave a tall, olive skinned police officer in his forties came out of an office and said.

"Come in here." The two looked at each other and followed him into the small office with one desk, two filing cabinets and four chairs. In passable English the officer said.

"You change English money for our money?"

"No," replied Bob, "that's against the law, it's illegal we wouldn't do that." He glanced at a worried looking Sam.

"I know you do, all you people on the site do it, I have been told."

"Nooo," they both shook their heads together now thinking they would be arrested very soon and put in the jail that Peter Hilton was resident in for three months. The officer put his hand in the back pocket of his trousers and pulled out a large amount of local currency and said.

"I go to England soon for a holiday, I give you thirty Dinar to one English pound, I take whatever you have got!"

*

Sam and Bob had been told by Hamid that they could pick up cheap toys and balloons from a market stall in the town close to the site at Barna, with Christmas day being on the following Wednesday the two made for the Friday market to purchase the goods.

It had turned cold over the past few days, and as they were a lot higher at this site, they had been told it was possible there could even be snow.

The two walked down from the site. The market was in a lower area of the town from where they had come. The white canvas roofs of the market stalls could be seen fluttering in the wind as they approached.

There were many stalls within the market, selling many different items, from colourful clothes, food, drink, household goods, live animals along with many other articles. There were smells from fresh cooking and other items and of course the toys. Within the market there were three rows of stalls, ten to each row which were close to each other, it was packed with locals at the time they had chosen to go.

Sam as always when away from site was totally covered from head to toe in her local dresses and headscarves with just her face exposed. Bob had gone to the next stall to look at some trousers. The female was totally engrossed in picking some small toys when a group of six women dressed from head to toe in black smock like dresses with their faces all covered apart from their eyes passed behind her in a line, led by a male at the front and one at the rear. It made Sam jump as one of the middle females bumped into her.

"Can you believe that? One of those bloody women just walked straight into me," she told Bob when he returned.

"Are you okay?" He asked.

"Yeah, I wasn't even moving, I had my back to her and, BANG, she nearly took me out!"

"Well," came the reply from the male, "I saw it as I was walking back, she did in fact go out of her way to knock into you, then the chap at the back shouted and pushed them all on."

"Oh, how odd," she felt her leather handbag which was on a long strap of the same material around her neck and one arm, hanging in front of her, "she wasn't after my handbag, well she didn't get it, even if she was."

"How's the toy buying coming on?"

"Oh, ok," she pointed to a heap of toys on the stall in front of her, "I think these will be ok, I think I have the right amount, I just want to get Fabi a hair brush and comb set before we leave here." She talked to the stall holder in French saying, "I will have these please, J'aurai ces jouets s'il vous plait," who walked around the stall with a light blue and white striped carrier bag, and put the items in it, Sam paid and thanked him. "Merci Monsieur," he nodded his thanks. "I think this lot will do. Oh, that bloody woman hurt my back," she rubbed the small of her back at the base.

"Come on, let's get going, bloody hell," Bob continued as he rubbed the left-hand side of his face, "I've got a toothache, it started this morning."

"Come on, you can pop into the medic when we get back to the base camp at Regama this afternoon."

*

"Can you believe it?" Bob said to Sam as the two stood in front of the notice board in the canteen on Christmas Day morning with other workers around them, they were looking at a notice that appeared that morning, it read,

Dear colleagues,

As I am sure you are aware that in your contract it reads that UK public holidays will be worked while you are in the country as these are not celebrated here. But as a show of good will, we are happy for you to have the 25th of December (Christmas Day) off.

You will be expected to return to work the following day, the 26th December at 7/00am and Friday the 28th in-lieu of having Christmas Day off. This has been relayed to us from the UK head office. Each worker will be given 2 bottles of local beer and half a bottle of wine to go with their Christmas dinner at 6/00 pm this evening.

Happy Christmas.
Hugh Cameron.
Project Manager.

"No Boxing Day off," moaned a worker from behind Bob, "and I have been told they are having seventeen days off in the head office at home."

"Oh," laughed Bob, as he half turned, "but you are getting beer and wine as compo."

"Big deal," the worker replied, "we don't get the UK bank holidays because they are not celebrated here, but we don't get the local public holidays either, they have nine in all!"

"Well," Bob turned around and said, "and we have to work Friday for no extra pay to make up for having today off!"

"Bloody hell yeah, thieving bastards." Bob was trying to think of something else to wind the worker up with, when the safety officer said.

"Come on, it's time to start getting the food down to the orphanage," as she pulled him away by the arm.

"Oh, I was just starting to enjoy that," Bob said as the two entered the kitchen."

"I know," replied Sam, "I could see a fight breaking out. Come on let's get the food. Oh, that turkey smells lovely."

The two had managed to collect loads of extra food for the orphanage, they got hold of three extra turkeys, there was plenty of vegetables to use, and the chefs had also cooked Christmas puddings and mince pies for the children and as they left, Harry the chef gave Sam three boxes of Christmas crackers to put out. The chefs also gave them a large amount of cooked wild boar that they had brought off the local chief of police, who had shot it the day before close to the town.

Bob and Sam had also invited Hamid and his wife Lilia, a plump thirty-year-old woman. They loaded everything that had been covered in tin foil into two vans and made their way down the hill to the home. Sam went in first. All the children were playing in the rear playground apart from Fabi who was, as always, sat reading by the rear doors, it was the book Sam had given her. The smile on the young child's face told the safety officer how pleased she was to see her.

Sam took Fabi outside with the others to play. As soon as this happened Bob, Hamid, Lilia and four workers were called in by Anya. It was only a matter of minutes before the whole dining room had been transformed into a festive scene. With of course red and white bunting tape running around and across the ceiling, and bundles of balloons hanging from different areas of the said ceiling. The large table was almost covered with the amount of food now on it. And to finish it all off Bob had managed to get hold of a would-be Christmas tree and had decorated it like the one in the canteen at Moura, when all was complete Anya called the children and other helpers in.

"Joyeux Noel, Happy Christmas!!!" In French was called out by everyone in the room as those from outside came in to take in what was before them. Most of the children were walking around with their mouths open as they could not comprehend what had gone on in the room in the short time since they were last in there.

The first thing which was completed, was the pulling of the Christmas crackers so that the children and workers could wear the paper hats while eating. It was with much excitement that this happened as the children had never done this before. With Fabi sitting on her chair and a cracker in each hand she pulled one with both Sam and Bob at the same time, then wore her bright red hat. It was at this point Fabi pointed to the ceiling and asked in English.

"What this is Mr Bob?"

"What is this?" Corrected Sam.

"What is this Mr Bob?"

"We call it Christmas Fabi, it is to celebrate when the baby Jesus, the son of God was born."

"Oh," came the reply, "I have written about this."

"No," corrected Sam, "you have read about this."

"Yes, I have read this Mr Bob." Bob hugged the young girl and kissed her on the cheek, with tears in his eyes he said.

"Happy Christmas Fabi."

"Joyeux Noel Mr Bob and Miss Sam."

There was much joy after the mid-day lunch. Sam handed out the toys which they had wrapped in brown paper from Colin in the office. While Fabi got a toy, she was also given the hair brush, comb and small looking glass set that Sam had bought her.

Games were played with much screaming and noise being made by everyone. Such as Blind Man's Bluff, Hide and Seek, Pin the Tail on the Donkey and much more.

A cassette radio had been set up and was playing Christmas songs. And as if by order Fabi pointed out of the window to show everyone that a small amount of snow was falling.

Fun and games went on all afternoon and it was almost four pm when a very drunk looking Hugh Cameron turned up with Colin for the photos to be taken. When everything was complete and the clearing up was ongoing Hugh approached Bob and Sam with Colin behind him and said.

"You know this isn't the end of it," he slurred, once again the two getting a full blast of a 10-year-old malt whisky from his growling mouth. "I will sort you pair of fuckers out."

"Come on Hugh," said Colin from behind him, "let's go back to the camp for Christmas dinner."

"NO," he snarled again, "these two have just totally taken the piss out of me, well I can tell you, no one takes the piss out of Hugh Cameron." Colin gently pulled at the project manager's right elbow.

"Come on Hugh, let's go."

"Colin fuck OFF," he pulled his arm away, "this want's sorting once and for all."

"Look Hugh," Bob put his two hands up in front of his chest, "we've had a good day for the kids, and you helped sort it, let's not spoil it, please," he pleaded.

"It's you two," he drunkenly pointed at them, "I've never hit a woman in all my life, but I have no problem giving you a punch in the face." He told Bob.

"That's not a wise thing to do Hugh," replied Bob.

"Oh, you think your fucking hard do you LAD?" He shouted at Bob.

"No, I am not, far from it, but I know someone who is."

"Oh, you fucking wanker, what you're going to get someone to do me are you?" Hugh took a very drunken swing towards Bob's face, before it was within two foot of its target, Sam's hand came from nowhere and caught the fist in mid flow in the palm of her hand. Hugh had total surprise on his face, then before anymore could happen he was dragged backwards by Colin and two other workers who without any more ado, removed him from the dining room then off the premises.

"You've done it again Miss Crisp, just as I was about to give him a good kicking," laughed Bob.

"I didn't want your lovely face to get messed up again," she kissed him on the lips.

"Oh, he might just have knocked this bloody," he rubbed the side of his face, "aching tooth out."

"Right, first thing in the morning you are going to the medic and get it sorted."

"Yes, Miss Crisp, come on, it's our turn to eat."

"Your right, but let's get back to the Regama camp."

"Your right, Hugh is going to be a lot less happy with us once it gets around what a woman has just done to him," smiled Bob in reply.

As the pair were about to get in their van Colin came down the hill after sending Hugh back to the site with the others.

"Look," he started as he approached them, "there won't be any need to report what just happened, I mean with Hugh trying to hit you that is?" Realising that they were now in a strong position and of course they had no intention of reporting him, Sam said.

"Well the thing is Colin we were just saying we should report it." Then catching on quickly to where she was going with it, her boyfriend added.

"And with Sam being the safety officer, well really, we have got no choice, have we?"

"Look, Bob, Sam. Hugh is in for the vacant 'stream managers' job, and is looking good for it. I will have a word with him and well, I know he has never been nice to you two, but I promise that will change, he does listen to me."

"Well," the female looked at the male and said, "what do you think Bob, it was you he tried to hit?"

"Only if he does change towards us, I mean that is a sackable offence, what happened there, gross misconduct, and he does abuse both of us every time he sees us."

"I will see that he does, and if you need any help over anything, you know, just give me a shout and we can get it sorted."

"Okay," came the joint reply as they shook hands with the office manager. When Colin was out of ear shot Sam shook Bob's hand and with a smile said.

"That was a result we were not expecting today Mr English."

"Indeed, Miss Crisp, not expected at all, what a nice Christmas present. Joyeux Noel Miss Crisp Joyeux Noel." He gently cupped both her cheeks in the palms of both his hands and kissed her lips.

Chapter 13

And the earth moved.

"I can get you down to the dentist in the town Bob," Jenson the medic, looked at his wrist watch, as he sat behind his desk in the large medical centre at the Regama base camp with Bob in a chair at the opposite side. "I think they open at nine thirty," said the muscular, tall, fair haired Welshman from Swansea. "You will have to pay in local money, I think it will cost about forty Dinar."

"That's not a problem," came the reply, as he got out of the chair.

"Come back about nine and I will get you down there."

"Oh," Bob rubbed the side of his face, "I can't wait to get it out." He turned and walked towards the door.

"Oh, Bob, there is one thing you should know."

"What's that Jenson?" Asked the man with the throbbing face.

"You do know they reuse needles here?"

"WHAT?"

"They do it all the time, I can take a needle down there for you, but the chance of that going in your mouth, well let's just say you've got more chance of winning the football pools without doing them."

"Bloody hell," he rubbed his face again, "what with all this AIDS thing."

"Well maybe that's one of the reasons it is so rife in Africa. Look, when do you go on leave next?"

"The middle of next month, it's about three weeks away."

"Look Bob, it's not worth chancing it, I can give you plenty of painkillers."

"And I can get my Mum to book me an appointment for the Monday after I get home, okay I'll do that, wow I am pleased you knew that."

"No problem."

"Oh, Jenson, can I use your phone, please, it's an in-country call."

"Yeah, help yourself, I've got to go to the office," the medic got up and left Bob to it.

*

Bob had his tooth extracted, a lower right molar on the first Monday that he returned home on leave after many weeks of pain. As they were only home for two weeks Bob and Sam took his girls to Central London for the middle weekend from the Friday to Monday and stayed in a West End hotel. As it was still pantomime season, on the Saturday afternoon they went to see Aladdin, and spent a few hours shouting, "he's behind you," and "oh no you won't," and other such things.

"When are you and Daddy getting married?" Lynn asked Sam has her and her sister sat in a restaurant, with the girlfriend of their father, who had excused himself to use the lavatory, once they had finished their meal after the theatre.

"Oh, well." The adult female could not finish her sentence as she was interrupted by the older sister Karen who asked.

"Mummy said she thinks you and Daddy will have a baby, are you having a baby Sam?" The sudden turn of conversation took the safety officer completely by surprise, and as she did pride herself of being able to say the correct thing at the right time, she delayed her reply by wiping her mouth with her napkin to gain more thinking time, then continued.

"Well, to the second question, no we will not be having a baby. How did this come up with your Mummy?"

"I heard her say to Auntie Jackie at the kitchen door," Karen put on an adults voice that made Sam smile, "I bet Bob and that bloody woman have a baby before you know it. I will go mad, as I wanted another one, and he said, no, we can't afford it."

"Do you not want babies?" Asked Lynn. Sam decided she would not discuss her lifelong medical history with two young ladies whom would no doubt then pass it on to their Mother, albeit unwittingly, so instead she replied.

"If Daddy and I did get married, and he has to ask me first," the three females nodded, "then I will have two lovely step daughters with both of you."

"Why will we be stepped on?" Asked Lynn.

"Oh, I will explain that at another time." Sam replied.

"We have chosen our bridesmaid dresses, they are pink," said Karen, "we saw them when out with Mummy, but she didn't know we were looking, did she Lynn?" Her sister nodded as she sucked on the straw in her glass of lemonade.

"Well, young ladies, let's just keep all that to ourselves for the time being." The two nodded their agreement.

"Keep what to yourselves?" Asked their father as he rounded the corner near them.

The three all smiled and the young ones followed the older one, as she tapped the side of her nose and they all said together, "girls talk Mr English, girls talk!"

*

They were traveling south to a site at Contina in the very hot July sun, they had not been to the site before, it had been going for some time, but as it was so far south they had not visited there to this point. But the site had been experiencing a lot of labour problems. They had been asked to go there by the new 'stream manager,' Hugh Cameron who now seemed to be their new best friend since the incident on Christmas Day. Colin had also moved with him to the other stream and it was to him Bob had mentioned about the "wreck of an old van they had," then low and behold there was a smaller newer model waiting for them on their return from the UK. This was along with a letter each from payroll saying they had both been awarded a salary increase on the recommendation of the 'stream manger.'"That will have been Colin," observed Sam.

"Yes, your right Miss Crisp, and it will have killed Hugh having to do it.," laughed Bob.

"It can't be much further now," said Sam as she looked at the map on her lap.

"It seems to have been forever, and there is nothing but the road and sand," replied the driver.

"Look," pointed the navigator, "that must be the town." An amount of white buildings came into view, with a heat haze above them.

"Are you sure it's not a mirage?" Smiled the driver. It was the town, they were not seeing things and it was not long before they found the large site at the other side of the town. The site was the same size as the Regama base camp, Tamra and Barna and while it had been running for over nine months progress had been slower than other sites, mainly because of its geography, being so far to transport materials, goods etc.

It was mid-afternoon that they arrived at the camp, but it was decided for Bob to have a meeting with project manager Ben McCleod, a tall well-built, dark haired fifty-eight-year-old Scotsman from Aberdeen, to find out what were the main issues, then meet with the lads the next day.

Sam was going to have her walk round inspection that afternoon then meet with Ben the next morning.

They decided to drop their things in their port-a-cabin first. They were given the keys and room number and pointed towards it by the camp boss. The accommodation area was behind the offices, canteen and bar set up, which had a swimming pool at the front of them. Many cabins made up the camp but Sam and Bob had been allocated a staff cabin which was larger than the workers rooms, while it still had two beds it also had its own shower and toilet area in which they had both said they were going to have a shower before doing anything else, to cool down.

It was Bob who was going to shower first, before his meeting. He made for the shower room which was across the far end of the room with a central door which had a bed and bedside cabinet each side and a window over the right-hand bed. With just a towel around his waist and flip-flops on his feet carrying his wash bag, he entered the rear room, shut the door then after a few seconds came running out shouting. "SNAKE, SNAKE, SNAKE," followed behind by the creature, he and Sam jumped onto the right-hand bed while the hissing snake disappeared under the left hand one. "Shit," was the comment from the man with a towel around his middle.

"Where did that come from?" Asked the female.

"It was curled up inside the shower cubicle."

"Well," said Sam, "we are going to have to get him out, we need help," she looked at her almost naked boyfriend and said, "it will have to be me, you won't get far like that."

"Ok, I'll wait here."

"I won't be long darling," she kissed him on the lips then got off the bed to head for the main door which had a wardrobe on each side of it. She had hardly made two steps on the floor when the snake's head appeared from under the side of the other bed not far from Sam and hissed at her, she was back on the bed in one leap to grab hold of Bob. "Bloody hell!"

"We are stuck here," replied Bob. "Can we get out of the window?" Without giving an answer, Sam opened it from the bottom and put the two opening arms at each side in place to leave a large open area, and said.

"See you soon," she kissed him again then almost head first disappeared out of the window.

"Bye, see you later," he said to the pair of disappearing soles from her boots.

Bob sat on the bed with his legs up for what seemed an age until Sam called through the window.

"Bob, Bob," the male climbed up to the window to see Sam and a slim, tanned, five-foot tall, long ginger haired forty-year Liverpudlian dressed only in blue shorts and brown boots. "This is Billy the Snake, the camp boss said he will sort it."

"Hi Bob," he said in a very strong Liverpool accent, as he put his hand up for Bob to shake, "got a little visitor I am told?"

"You could say that," came a half laughing reply, "you'd better be careful."

"No problem Bob lad, we'll soon have him sorted," he held up a round stick about one inch in diameter and two foot long. He disappeared then within seconds the main door opened and Billy entered the room with Sam at the door behind him, "where is the little bugger then?"

"He's under there," Bob pointed to the next bed. Billy hit the top of the bed with the stick, and the snake's head appeared hissing again, within a flash the stick went sideways at the far end from Billy into the snake's mouth which the hissing intruder bit down on.

"Got yah," smiled the snake catcher as he pulled the fighting creature from under the bed with its tail rattling and grabbed hold of the other end. "Wow, aren't you a big fellow, a Carpet Viper if I am not mistaken? Five-foot-long I would say," he looked from the intruders head to tail, "come in love," he called over his shoulder to Sam, "he's fine, I've got him, it's no problem." Sam came in and stood by the wardrobe, and was joined by Bob from the bed.

"How do you know so much about snakes?" Asked Bob, "there's not many in Liverpool."

"Oh, there's plenty of snakes in the Pool lad," laughed Billy, "but not this kind. No, it's me Pa, he has an exotic pet shop at home, I was brought up with this kind of thing, and I have worked in Africa for a fair few years now."

"How did it get in here?" Asked Sam.

"It's the bloody local cleaners we have here love, always leaving the doors open, and the snakes, they just slip in, that's if they are not nicking your gear, the cleaners that is, not the snakes. Ali Bar-Bars as they call them here," Billy laughed. "Don't leave anything laying around while you're here, lock it in your wardrobes. The last time I was home I brought back loads of bars of laxative chocolates and one at a time I left one beside my bed. That cleaner of ours must have spent half her life on the shitter, but she kept taking them," he laughed, "it is funny as she wouldn't have had a clue way she was going all the time."

"Will you kill him?" Bob pointed at the snake.

"Nooo! Never, no, I will take him down to the long grass at the far end of the site and let him go there. I would take him home for Pa if I could, I would get good money for him, but you'd never get him through customs. No, I will just stick with the tortoises."

"Tortoises?" Asked Bob.

"Oh yeah, take two or three little baby ones in each jacket pocket every time I go on leave, I can get them for next to nothing here and get a fortune for them at home these days."

"Have you never been stopped?" Asked Sam.

"No, not yet love, if they did find them they would be so busy with them, I don't think they would find the two or three ounces of weed I carry inside the jacket. Right can't talk all day, got to let this chap go then I'll be back for that little fellow," he nodded towards the floor, "I'll get a small box I've got in my room and he can come home with me next time."

"What little fellow?" Asked a puzzled Bob.

"Him," Billy nodded again towards the floor and the corner of the wardrobe, "the scorpion, got to go." He turned and left the room. The two looked closer at the scorpion which they had not seen up until that point, then looked at each other and both screamed.

"SCORPION!!!" And both jumped back onto the bed.

*

Sam and Bob were sitting in the packed canteen eating breakfast the following morning at a six-seater table with their backs to the service area and entrance door when a head appeared between the two of them and said, "I would know these two lovely people anywhere in the world." They both looked at the person and cried out together.

"Wolfie!!!" The two jumped up and the three hugged at the same time.

"Didn't know you were here Wolfie," said Bob.

"Well in fact," they all sat down at a table, "I haven't been on this site long, but I have been out here over six months now, just come back from leave and got moved here."

"Did you sort the kitchen out at home?" Asked Sam.

"Oh, the wife divorced me over it."

"Nooo," came the joint surprised reply.

"No, only joking, no I sorted it all out, she's fine now. I did hear that a male and female turned up on site yesterday and were shut in their room by a snake," he laughed.

"Hold on," put in Bob, he held his arms out, "a bloody big one."

"Five-foot-long Billy the Snake said," continued Sam.

"And a scorpion," put in Bob.

"Those kinds of things are everywhere here," Wolfie continued, "and packs of wild dogs, they roam around the outside of the site. And we have," he motioned the other two in, then in a soft voice said, "and we have packs of wild Scotsman that do the same thing."

"We need to talk, Wolfie," Bob said, "we have been told there are problems to sort out." Wolfie just nodded then said.

"Look Bob lad, we have got a big pour of concrete to get started, I am off now. You two finish your breakfast then come and find me in an hour or so," he stood up, "lovely to see you both, and don't be getting yourselves caught by any little snakes or spiders again," he laughed. As he did that a fly popped on a nearby fly trap, "three," he remarked.

"Don't tell me you count the dead flies' as well Wolfie?" Asked Bob.

"Oh yes lad, the first beer of the night is on it."

"That's a worry," put in Sam, "I mean the thing you look forward to most in a day is how many flies' have died."

"It is that lass, it is indeed. I'll see you later," the big man turned and walked away.

"There he is," Bob pointed towards Wolfie, who was stood on a ground floor slab which had steel reinforcement in it and a mobile crane by the side that had a concrete skip on it, which when full would hold half a metre of concrete from the six-metre concrete truck which was stood to one side of the floor slab. Wolfie was directing the crane driver to where the skip was needed. Apart from a very small pair of underpants he was only wearing a pair of wellington boots. He had another four workers with him, all of them had shorts on along with their wellies.

"He is very red," commented Sam, "and nearly naked I may add." The two stood on the road that overlooked the area which would be the base for an accommodation block. Once he had emptied the skip he pointed to the other workers what to do then. After putting his shorts on and lighting a cigarette, he then took a drink of water out of the insulated water container and made his way up the dried out muddy bank to join the others. The sun was rising in the cloudless sky and the temperature was already becoming extremely hot.

"Glad you put the shorts on Big Man," smiled Bob when he had joined them.

"My wife said in her last letter that our five-year lad was asked by his school teacher, 'what does your Daddy do in Algeria?' And he said, 'he works in his underpants.'" They all laughed at this comment.

"Your skin is very red Wolfie," the safety officer observed, "and you have been out here sometime now?"

"Just can't go brown, Sam lass."

"Does it hurt?" Asked Bob.

"No not at all, I have spent a fortune on sun oils over the years, but this is it," he held his arms out and did a twirl, "like a tomato, bright red." Said the man from the north east of England. "Just the same when I worked in Uganda."

"Be careful," replied Sam, "I read an article a little while ago about too much sun being connected to skin cancer."

"Oh, I am fine lass. Have you seen our general foreman Don Trill, now he has been here a long time and his face is just grey, no colour at all?"

"We are meeting with him later," put in Sam, "over some safety matters."

"Well, that's just one of the problems. A load of the lads are fed up with that Don, Ben McCleod and all the ground workers, they come from the same area, up there," he pointed to the sky, the other two looked up. "Scotland, they all worked together in the UK, they get away with murder, come and go as they like. Got three cabins next to each other, six of them. They call the cabins, 'Happy Valley' it's party night every night there, and they come to work at any hour. Yet for the rest of us, Don Trill is standing at the gate outside the canteen at seven every morning, and if any of us are late, well, you get your time docked."

"That doesn't sound good," commented Bob.

"No," came the reply, "and Don messes with our overtime hours all the time, and they have another lad, of theirs, who is a night watchman. We often have the site robbed by the locals living around here, so Peter, that's his name, has a crew of local watchmen he oversees. I hear he is on time and a half all of the time, as he works nights, and every night he is pissed, goes around all the cabins where drinking is going on and gets arseholed."

"Bloody hell," came the joint reply.

"Look, I've got to get back to work. It's Thursday night, I have got the three of us an invite to the fitters, welders and sparks (electricians) bar-b-q tonight, they have one every Thursday night outside their cabins, they have a good set up. They brew their own beer and wine. it's a good night, singing songs and all," he started to walk away, "I'll see you there at half seven." He then returned down the bank to his work.

*

For the rest of the day Sam made out reports and checked to see if her list was being attended to. She also talked to many of the lads about care of their skin in the high temperatures, and sent a few who seemed to have skin issues to the medic.

Bob meet with other workers to hear stories that backed up Wolfie's account of what was going on, he finished the day with a meeting between himself, the project manager and general foreman, who rejected the allegations levelled at them, putting it down to, "jealousy, because of the friendship between themselves and the ground workers." Bob left the meeting thinking that there was truth in what he had been told by the other workers but at the same time was left wondering what was the best way forward, but he did have a confidante in Sam with whom he would discuss the matter later.

The pair turned up a little later than the others for their evening out but had no problem with finding the party as it was just a case of following the music and smell of cooking. The welders had cut two 45-gallon diesel drums long ways in half, welded steel reinforcement bars to them for legs and grills to cook the food on. There was a large area outside the last two cabins in the camp which they had set up the cooking area along with flood lights, music speakers, chairs and tables and even a small bar for everyone to get a homemade drink from.

"This is like being on holiday," commented Bob to Wolfie as they ate burgers and other food. Sam and Bob agreed they would not stay long as they had a long drive the next day between them. When the food had been cleared away they had a guest appearance from Peter the night watchman. He appeared to have visited a few other parties that were going on around the camp beforehand, with a bottle of beer already in hand the stocky thirty-five-year-old, fair haired and bearded face Scotsman gave a rendition of a song he had made up to the tune of the hunting song, 'John Peel.'

"Do ye ken Don Trill with his face so grey?
Do ye ken Don Trill at the break of each day?
Do ye ken Don Trill when he's far, far away?
But he'll be at the gate in the morning."

This brought great roars of laughter from all of those attending the gathering, Peter held his arms in the air then took his bow's, then with a bottle of home-made wine he was given, he staggered off to his next appearance at another party.

"He's a good laugh," said Wolfie to Sam and Bob, "and he does go into lads' rooms at night and tells them bedtime stories, but it is a worry that it's him who is protecting us from getting murdered in our beds!"

"With that sobering thought," Bob said as he got up, "I think we will be off as we have a long way to go tomorrow." The two bid their goodnights, farewells and thanks, then returned to their room, both armed with large sticks they had picked up on the way, to fend off any uninvited guests that may have been waiting in their room, but after a search, all was clear. They then undressed and jumped in the same bed together, with Bob asking, "was it time to make some mummy and daddy noises?"

They woke up in each other's arms some hours later as Sam said.

"Oh, Mr English, you have made the earth move for me."

"And you for me Miss Crisp." They said no more as the trembling grew stronger.

"That's more than an earth termer Bob," items started to fall off the shelves, the wardrobes were rocking from side to side as the portable cabin was shaking fiercely.

"Bloody hell Sam get up, it's an earthquake." The two jumped out of the right-hand bed and got dressed as fast as they could in the rocking room, after what seemed a complete age the shaking subsided. They opened the door to see other workers coming out of their rooms when they heard a shout of.

"A cabin has been swallowed into the ground." Bob and Sam ran into the middle of the camp in the darkness, all power had disappeared as the generators had been knocked out by the quake, it was now only a bright moon in a cloudless sky that lit the way.

When they arrived to where the shouts had come from the sight that greeted them was one of complete horror. A double ended unit (a room at each end for two people) had snapped off a row of eight and all that could now be seen was about two foot sticking out of the ground with a door in it.

There was a lot of chaos and many male workers were staggering around mainly in their underwear making a lot of noise, most of them the worse for wear through alcohol. After a short while of her and Bob trying to calm everyone down, Sam took control of the situation by shouting out very loudly.

"Everyone, shut the fuck up, NOW!" A pin could now have been heard, had it dropped. "Right, we need silence to work out who's in there and how we are going to get them out." Bob moved towards the cabin, there was a very large crack in the ground running from where the cabin had gone down. "Be careful Bob," said Sam as she held his hand.

"Let me find out who's in there?"

"Be careful," he made his way as near as he dared, when about three metres away he shouted.

"Who's in there, how many of you are there?"

"There's two of us here, but there are two at the other end in their room," came the north of England accent reply. At that point the cabin slipped a small amount more, Bob instinctively jumped back to safety. At this point they were joined by Wolfie who was wearing just very tight, brief blue underpants.

"Be careful of aftershocks lass," advised the newcomer, "I got caught out by one in, oh aha, yes the Sudan."

"Ok, thanks Wolfie. RIGHT!" She shouted, "we need a crane driver, who's preferably not drunk."

"That's me," a tall black-haired man with a beard in his forties from Derby came forward with his hand up, "Steve the crane Harwood," he shook hands with Sam, "what do you want?"

"We need you to set your crane up, 'Steve-the-crane,' as close as you can, if we have to move cabins that's what we will do. We will get your chains on the end of the cabin, when you have got the weight of the unit we get the lads out then we try to pull it out."

"I am on it," said Steve, as he turned and disappeared.

"Okay," she continued in a loud voice, "we need light, who can get these flood lights working?" She pointed to the dead lights on top of the cabins which had not moved.

"That's me," a stocky forty-five-year-old from Devon, "Joey the Sparks."

"Thanks Joey the Sparks," the safety officer replied. "Okay," she shouted again, "we need a ladder, the length of one unit, a few scaffold boards to get across to it, and rope. We are going to get the first two lads out, then lift the unit out to rescue the others."

Before another word could be spoken, the aftershock that had been forecast by Wolfie arrived. Everyone stood still as the earth shook lightly for just a few seconds. When all was calm again the safety officer repeated her instructions. Men started to move off saying they would "get this and that."

"I think, we will need a wood saw," Sam said to Bob, "we may need to cut through the double thick plywood wall to get the other lads out if we can't pull the unit out"

"I've got one in my room, I will get it," said a voice from behind her.

"Thanks," she called over her shoulder.

"Is there anything I can do Sam lass?" Asked Wolfie from beside her. She looked him up and down, then replied.

"Yes, go and make yourself decent!"

As fast as everyone moved it did take some time to have everything in place to start retrieving the workers and cabin from out of the void that had opened up.

Dawn was starting to break as Joey the Sparks got the flood lights back on. No other cabins had to be moved for the crane to reach the stricken unit, but Steve had to extend the complete jib of his mobile crane.

Four chains of the set that hung from the cranes block were attached to fixing points on each corner of the unit so that the crane could take the weight, and that it could not slip any more. But as Steve carried out the operation, warning bells began ringing in his crane to warn him that he was on his maximum weight, which could tip it over, at this point Wolfie who was now decent said.

"I'll get a forklift and put some of the ton precast concrete panels on the back of the crane that will hold it down." When all of that had been completed Bob placed four scaffold boards doubled up across the void onto the cabin then crawled across and fitted a chain on each corner. Once this was complete he opened the door then passed a ladder inside which had been passed to him, for the first two occupants to climb out.

"Let's try and lift it out," said Sam once the scaffold board had been removed. Directions were given to Steve by a banksman who was standing on top of a cabin so he could see the driver and unit at the same time. Very slowly, inch by inch the unit was pulled out until it was laid safely onto the ground. At this point they were joined by the project manager who had seemed to have just woken up.

"Well done everybody," he gave out his congratulations.

"It was Sam who sorted it all out, had us all running everywhere, telling us what to do, she was a real hero," said Wolfie as he re-joined them.

"Well done young lady," Ben was about to shake her hand when the door opened to the end room that had just been pulled out to show Peter the night-watchman. "What were you doing in there?" Ben snapped at Peter.

"It's my room Ben."

"I know it's your room, but you were meant to be working, was you in there sleeping?"

"Nooo, no, I just popped in to get some smokes," he took a pack out of the top pocket of his sleeveless checked shirt and held them in the air, and said "I've been guarding the site Ben."

"Right Peter, we will have words later." The guard turned and made a hasty retreat.

"Right," said Sam to Bob so only he could hear, "come with me, we need to make the earth move again after all THAT!"

Chapter 14

The Ends in Sight.

"Oh, wow, this is a surprise!" Sam sat on the side of her bed facing Bob who was in the same position on the one opposite her, in their room, reading their mail the evening they had returned to the base camp after being away for some weeks.

After the problems they had found at Contina, they had a meeting with Hugh Cameron and Colin who had wasted no time in splitting up the ground workers and sending them to different sites, along with Don the general foreman and Peter the night watchman, who had also been given a final written warning for drinking on duty. They had then spent some months moving around the country. "I have been offered a new job."

Bob looked up from his own letter and asked, "where, when, how, who?"

"A lot of questions Mr English."

"Yes, I know, but I have a surprise also, but you go first."

"Oh, right, hmm, well it's from Johnston, who I used to work for, it's my old boss, he had heard I was coming to the end of my contract and has offered me the safety managers position for their southern region. I would have four safety officers under me."

"Wow, well done, we hadn't really talked about what we were both thinking of doing at the end of this contract, I mean staying or going?"

"How do you feel Bob?"

"Well, the thing is, I just miss my girls so much. I know I won't be at home with them, but if I was in the UK I would go to court should I have to, to say get them every weekend or so, how would that be with you?"

"I think we have just about agreed that you are moving in with me when we do go home, we have spent a fair bit of time together now, and haven't killed each other," he nodded his agreement with a smile. "I would love to have the girls as much as possible, I think they are lovely, just like their father. Now what's your news?"

"Well, I don't want to steal your thunder, BUT, it just so happens that you are not the only one to be offered a new job."

"Wow, tell me more?"

"It's an old mate of mine, Alan Hoddle, he's not a builder as such, but more of a developer, he buys land, gets builders to build the houses, then he sells them."

"You don't build houses."

"No, but I am a builder, done it all of my life, house building is the easy end of our industry, how hard can it be? Get your head around it and away you go."

"I am sure a lot of house builders would not agree with you Bob?"

"Yes, no doubt you are right, again. But I have built some really complicated buildings, build a few houses and then they will more or less be the same, again and again, surely?" He held his arms out sideways.

"I do think you're right, so what is it with Alan?"

"I told him I would probably be moving out Kent way with you. He is buying some land out there, building four very big houses. He is going to build them himself, and he wants me to run the site for him, be his site manager."

"Wow, Bob, that would be a step up for you also, how do you feel about it, being a manager that is?"

"Well, I never saw myself as a manager years ago, but I must say, since I have been dealing with the lad's problems and everything, yes, I reckon I could do it."

"I know you could, and as long as you are open with the trades that it was your first manager's role, they would all help you along, I am sure of that. And I know a person can do a site mangers course now, so you could get another qualification along with your carpenters City & Guilds."

"Yeah, your right, that would be good. And if you take your job offer, well it would be a new start for both of us. I do think it's time to go home."

Sam got up and moved across the room and sat next to her boyfriend who put his arm around her, "and we could live happily ever after Mr English."

"We could indeed, Miss Crisp."

*

"There has been an accident." Bob and Sam were sitting in the stream managers office across the desk from James Hardwick, "it's down at the site, Hettino."

"Yes, we know it," said Sam, "we were there a few months ago, weren't we Bob?"

"Yes, it's one of the smaller sites." Replied her co-worker.

"Well," continued the stream manager, "this is not an ordinary accident, one of our workers," he looked down at some paperwork on the desk in front of him, "David Andrews, he's a roofer. It was last Friday afternoon when the lads were off work. He drove a minibus with some lads in, to go for a ride out. As they returned to their town, Hettino, it was getting dark and a local chap who was drunk walked out in front of the bus, killed straight away."

"Bloody hell," replied Bob, Sam put her hand over her mouth.

"There were loads of witnesses who said that the chap walked out and the police have cleared David of any wrongdoing."

"So, what's the problem?" Asked the safety officer.

"The problem is," James continued, "that his family is trying to get David to pay for their families living, I mean while his children are growing up, there's three young ones."

"Can they do that?" Asked Bob.

"Well, they have said it's a law here, we don't know, we have our solicitors in the UK looking into it. But it has been decided not to chance it and just get him out, it could become very complicated, also some of the locals have turned nasty about it, and were at the site looking for him the other day."

"Where do we come in?" Asked Bob.

"We are off to pick him up, aren't we James, we are the get-away-drivers?" Asked Sam.

"Well, yes, it was thought you are not known there, don't take your van, we have a car for you. He is booked on a flight to the UK tomorrow, Friday. You two need to get down there today, then early tomorrow morning, before it gets light would be good, get him out and up to the airport, okay?"

"Okay," said Sam, "we can do that."

"Dave, the office manager has a car sorted for you, it's full of fuel." The two got up and left the office with Bob collecting the car keys on the way, when out of earshot of everyone Bob said.

"We seem to get all the crap jobs."

"We do Mr English; indeed, we do, but we are out of here soon, with new jobs, and we have now got a car to drive, not that rotten old van. I baggies," she grabbed the keys out of his hand, then ran off backwards, holding the keys in the air, smiling then said, "first drive!"

*

Not only did Sam drive the car first but she did for the entire journey, which took approximately four hours, stopping once at a garage in the middle of nowhere for petrol for the return journey, more drinking water and a toilet break.

It was late in the afternoon and early evening with the sun going down that gave an orange glow above the site which was at the start of the town as it came into sight. The site at Hettino was larger than the one at Moura, again the large concrete wall had been erected early in the project for security reasons.

They met with David in the office, a tall slim dark haired forty-six-year-old man from Hereford. They agreed to have an early breakfast the next day then set off for the long drive to the capital and the afternoon flight to the UK.

"I can't believe this has happened," said David as he talked to Bob and Sam while the office manager Paul left the small office to continue sorting the exit papers.

"This job was going to be a new start for me and the family, save some money, start to buy our house off the council, now it's all gone. I haven't even done my first three months. I was out of work before coming here, now it will be back to the dole."

The two newcomers looked at each other as David held his head in his hands, and appeared to be weeping. They were looking for words of inspiration, but none were coming, then David sat up and wiped his eyes and continued by saying. "Most of all I have killed a man, there's me worrying about myself, and that poor man is dead."

"It's alright to worry about yourself and your family David," replied Sam, "don't beat yourself up."

"David, the man was drunk, there were witnesses, there was nothing you could do," put in Bob.

"Oh, it was awful, I wasn't even going fast, as people are always walking in the streets here." He wiped his eyes again, "he just appeared from nowhere, in fact," he took a deep breath then breathed out again, before he continued. "One of the lads who was in the front with me said he came out from behind one of those large orange trees they have beside the roads here."

"Ok, I have all the paperwork sorted out," said Paul the middle-aged short bald-headed Irishman as he entered the office. "As you are not a resident you do not need an exit visa so that saves telling the local police that you are going. Here's the keys for your room," he handed them to Sam.

"Can he not just be moved to another site?" Asked Bob.

"We looked at that" answered Paul, "we have to tell the authorities when we transfer someone within the country, so the local police would know and while he is in the country the family could make a claim, I am sorry but it is best he leaves, for his own good." The three stood up, Sam hugged David before she and Bob left the office.

After they found their room they headed for their evening meal in the canteen, bar, it's set up was like the one at Moura, but again bigger in size to accommodate the larger workforce.

It was later when the two of them sat to eat, most of the other workers had finished their meals and some of the lads started to move tables and chairs away stacking them around the external walls of the canteen.

"What's going on?" Asked Bob as the table was almost taken away with their plates still on them.

"It's horse racing night," replied one of the workers picking up one end of the table.

"Horse racing?" Asked Sam, "where do you keep them," she smiled.

"You'll see love, come on, we need to crack on, it starts soon." Before their eyes the canteen bar area was transformed into a cleared floor space which had a roll of fabric unrolled upon it. On the material six lines had been drawn long ways, and fourteen across. Each lane was numbered one to six, wooden cut-outs of horses had been placed on each lane, a table was set up to take bets. A dice would be rolled to confirm which lanes horse would move, then rolled again to indicate how many times. All the money taken was split between the gamblers of the winning horse.

"And the first spot prize of the night," shouted one of the two bookies who stood up behind the table wearing a bowler hat and holding a bottle of beer in the air. "For a bottle of the finest local beer, to the first person to answer this question correctly. Who won the English FA Cup in 1952?"

"I know, I know," came a reply of a Scottish accent from the centre door which had just opened.

"You know the rules, you need to come over and tell me," came the reply. The newcomer hurriedly made his way across the room and once at the table shouted out.

"Newcastle United!"

"Is correct," shouted the hatted bookie, as he handed the beer over to the man who held the bottle in the air to the cheers of the workforce, "and the first winner tonight is, Peter the night watchman!" Sam and Bob turned and looked at each other in total surprise as Bob said.

"I am really glad that final written warning worked then!"

*

Bob and Sam had returned to the base camp at Regama after their mercy dash to the airport and decided to go up to the site at Barna as they had not been there for a while and Sam wanted to see Fabi and take the children sweets, as they only had two weeks to go before they finished. They decided to go up on the Thursday evening and stay at the camp overnight then go to the Friday market for the sweets.

As they were about to leave the base camp Sam saw a female cleaner Zaza, outside the canteen that she always talked to in French, not only did Zaza have her face covered with her head scarf which was not only unusual but when Sam tried to talk to her she turned and ran away. Sam asked another cleaner, "what was that all about?" Then reported to Bob. "Apparently her husband gets drunk and beats her, he is doing it more of late, she does not want us to see her like it." She shook her head then continued, "Bob, can we help her?"

"I don't know, if we interfere it may make it worse for her."

"Yes, you're right, look give me five minutes I am going to find her and have a word."

"Ok, I will wait in the van." It was in fact over half an hour before Sam returned and entered the van to wake the sleeping and snoring Bob.

"I could hear your snores from the other side of the canteen," she smiled as Bob rubbed his eyes.

"Oh, how did you get on?" He yawned.

"I don't know. She has promised me she will go to the police if it happens again, but, aha, I don't think she will." As he started the van, Bob replied.

"Let's think about it, we may come up with something."

*

Things did not go completely to plan as when they passed the orphanage the children were outside playing and Fabi was propped against the wall on her crutches reading her French to English translation book. They stopped the van and joined the children.

"Hello Miss Sam and Mrs Bob, so love to see you," commented Fabi as she was joined by the pair after they had fought their way through the mob of children. They both hugged and kissed her before Sam corrected her English, then said.

"Your English is getting so good Fabi."

"I read your book each day," she held two fingers up, "for two hours Miss Sam and," she thought for a second, then nodded her head and said, "Mr Bob, as I cannot play with the others," she looked down at her legs, Sam hugged her again.

"Look we have to go to work now, but we will be back to see you tomorrow," Sam promised.

"With sweets," put in the male. This brought squeals of joy from both females who hugged again. As they started to drive to the site Sam said.

"We will have to tell her tomorrow we are leaving soon."

"Yeah, that's not going to be easy."

"I have been thinking Bob, could we not take her home with us, I mean adopt her, not just kidnap her one night," she smiled.

"Sam, I have thought about it, it would not be simple," he thought for a moment as the approached the site gates, "maybe when we get home we could try and put the wheels in motion with ours and their Embassy in London."

"Promise Mr English."

"I promise Miss Crisp." The female leant across and kissed the driver on his cheek.

After breakfast the following morning the two construction workers made their way to the market to buy the sweets and a few other gifts for the children early on so that they could spend most of their day off at the orphanage, that was after Bob popped into the office to make another phone call for the lads he had been helping with their paperwork problems.

They were both together in the packed market looking at sweets and filling bags with loose items when a line of women dressed fully in black, with only their eyes showing, with a man at the front of the group and one at the rear pushed their way through.

Sam took little notice of them until like the time before when they were in this market, one of the women bumped into Sam, before she could protest the women grabbed her hand then looked at her and slightly shook her head before being pushed on her way by the woman behind her.

"Bloody hell," said Bob, "that blinking woman bumped into you again." Sam put her finger to her lips, so as not to speak. The pair finished their shopping and made towards the van, without talking, when they were both in, with the male in the driving seat, a very puzzled Bob asked, "what is it?"

"She, the woman who bumped into me, put this in my hand," she held up a small piece of folded white paper, "I think it's a note."

"What does it say?" Sam opened it up and began to read out loud.

"*I am a British national from Scotland, I have been kidnapped from a Mediterranean island where I was working as a travel rep, and I am being kept as a slave. I am in the large white house with the light blue wall around it, with black iron gates in the street facing the road that runs up to the market.*

Don't go to the local authorities as some of them visit the house. Please help me."

Annabel Ferguson.

"Oh, my good God," replied the driver, "we were told about this sort of thing when we were in Greece with the girls."

"Bob, what are we going to do?"

Chapter 15

Show us your face.

They spent the rest of the day at the orphanage as planned, as they decided with it being a Friday it was not a good day to try to talk to anyone, but would go to see the stream manager at the Regama base camp the next morning, they decided it was best not to tell anyone at the Baran site as Bob said, "we don't want anyone to let the cat out of the bag." It was ten o'clock on the Saturday morning before they could get to see the manager James Hardwick.

"So, what do you think?" Asked Bob as he and Sam sat in the manager's office, in chairs facing him across his desk after explaining the situation.

"Well," he held the note in his hand after reading and thinking for a while, "do you think it's real, not someone just having a joke?"

"Nooo, no," stressed Sam, "I saw her eyes, I can assure you this is no joke."

"Look," came the reply, "let's say, well, look, we are guests in this country, the last thing we want to do is to." Before he could finish his sentence Bob broke in.

"The last thing we want to do is upset the local authorities, is that the case James?"

"Look Bob, we don't know what this girl has got herself into."

"She hasn't got herself into anything James," snapped the female.

"She's been fucking kidnapped!" Bob barked.

"Hold on Bob," the manager gestured with both hands pushing down, "just calm down."

"Calm fucking down," the workers liaison officer stood up, "right I'll tell you what James, I don't give a fuck who I upset, I know people in the British Embassy in the capital, I am," he snatched the note out of James hand across the desk, "going there now and see what they have to say about It."

"Bob," the manager stood up. "I must remind you that you are here on business for the company."

"Sack, me," came the reply.

"And me," said the safety officer as she also stood up. "And as soon as we get home, we will go to the newspapers and tell them what has happened here, and how you would not help this poor woman." There was total silence in the room as the manager thought about his next words carefully.

"Please sit down?" Said James, they all returned to their seats. "You are both out of here soon," they both nodded, "she is right, we can't go to the people here as, yes they nearly all know each other."

"Let us go to the embassy?" Said Sam.

"I can't let you go to the embassy."

"Why not?" Asked Bob.

"Let's, well, hmm, it's."

"Political," put in Sam, "we can't be upsetting people here."

"And don't forget, James," put in Bob, "she is from your part of the world, meaning Scotland."

"Right, this has got out of hand, first of all, it doesn't matter where she comes from, if this person is in need of help, well, yes we will help her." The manager took a deep breath, then blew it out, then continued. "We have to be careful how we do it. I mean no bull in a china shop stuff, and of course we don't want the people who are holding her to get wind of it and move her elsewhere."

"Totally agree," replied Bob, "we will play it your way James, but I really think we need to move as soon as possible."

"Okay," the manager stood up, "you have my blessing to go to the embassy, as you know people there, but you must keep me updated with your every move, ok?"

"Okay," they both said together, and shook hands across the desk, the pair then turned and left the office. Bob then phoned his contact at the embassy to tell him the news and to ask if they could come over, to which he was told they could, once in the van Sam asked?

"Are we really going to tell James our every move Bob?"

"Absolutely not, look we have got less than two weeks to go, I don't think he would tell people on purpose, but let's not chance it. We plan most of our own work."

"So, we keep away from here," smiled Sam, "and I have an idea, I will tell you on the way to the embassy." Sam then jumped with a start as there was a thump on her passenger window, she wound the window down to talk to Zaza the cleaner in French, when she finished she said to the male. "He beat her again last night, she is going to leave him and go to live with her parents, and then go to the police, she wants me to go with her"

"That's not a problem, let's sort this out then you can take her. Do you want me to come also?"

"I told her you would come."

"Thanks Sam!"

*

"I will not say this is a massive surprise," commented Bert Bartram the fifty-five-year-old, suited with dark blue tie, tall in height, grey haired diplomat, who sat across his wide desk in the British Embassy. "We have been told that there are gangs operating in the Med, taking young women and well, hmm, sold as, let's say, slaves."

"Well we have also been told about this before," put in Bob as the phone on the diplomat's desk rang, Bert picked it up and answered.

"Yes," he listened for a short while then said, "right, thank you for that," he put the hand set back in the phone's cradle. "After you rang me earlier, I gave our people at home Annabel's name to check it out, and yes, an Annabel Ferguson was reported missing over a year ago now, she disappeared on her day off, nothing heard of her since."

"Oh," Bob groaned as he rubbed his forehead.

"I have an idea," put in Sam, "if we go to the house it could go very wrong."

"Agreed," nodded the suited man.

"Look," she continued, "it seems that they go to the market most Fridays, when she sees me she comes my way. When I see them come in, I will get close and shout her name out, then, as long as she is there, Bob and I will grab her."

"You will need help, in case it goes wrong or turns nasty." Bert replied.

"In the background," said Bob, "not lots of police or army, that would only scare them off."

"No that's fine, I agree. I have a good contact here, but I will not tell him what it is for, just in case. Everyone seems to know everyone here within a few hundred miles or so. When are you going to do it?"

"We finish here next week, fly out on Tuesday, if we do it this Friday and get Annabel, she can come home with us," said Sam.

"That's fine, she can stay here, and I can get her tickets and documents sorted out. And I will sort everything else," he stood up, as did the others, "ring me on Thursday Bob, and hopefully we can action it for Friday. I will talk to my contact now and start getting things in place."

"Thank you, Bert," they all shook hands, "can I have a word with you, about the lad's papers and everything."

"Of course, sir."

"I'll see you in the van Sam."

"Oh, okay," Sam, feeling unwanted, turned and left the office.

*

That afternoon after they had been to the embassy they collected Zaza and then took her to her house, to collect her belongings before taking her to the police station, then on to her parent's house. Her husband was at work so there was no confrontation and the police said they would pick him up that night, after Zaza had given a statement with Sam by her side.

After they had unloaded her belongings from the van and were sitting in the front with Sam driving, Bob asked, "what do you think then Sam?"

"I don't know" came the reply as they drove off, "I am worried how her husband will react after he is taken in by the police."

"That's what I am concerned about."

"When I went in the house with her," the safety officer continued, "her father picked up a shotgun and said, 'if he comes here, I blow his fat head off.'"

"Oh, my good God," said Bob, holding his own head, "with this and Annabel, what in hell's name have we got ourselves into Sam?"

*

"They are coming," said Bob in a low voice, "don't turn around Sam, they have just entered the market." Bob had his back to the sweet stall where Sam, who was dressed in her local attire, with her head covered, was choosing sweets for the children.

"How many are there?" Came the reply.

"Not sure, about the same as before, it's about six women and a man back and front, I think they are going to come past us," he continued in a softer voice. "Hold on, they are passing the next stall, hold on, hold on, hold on, okay now." Sam turned around as the group singly filed past them, a slim woman near the middle walked into Sam.

"Anabel Ferguson?" Asked Sam, the woman stopped and looked at her but said nothing. "Anabel, is that you?"

"Hey, you fucking English," called the man from the rear, at this point all the women stopped as did the other male, "FUCK OFF," the rear male shouted, then screamed at the women to move in French, "BOUGE TOI, BOUGE TOI!!!"

"Anabel?" Asked Bob, "we are here to help you, if it's you show your face." The man at the rear pushed through the crowd to where the conversation was occurring.

"I told you English, FUCK OFF!" Sam looked at the female and pleaded.

"Anabel, please, please, we will save you." Before another word could be spoken Annabel pulled the hood from her head and the veil from her face at the same time to expose her shoulder length blond hair.

"YES, IT'S ME," she screamed, "there's three of us," at this point two of the other young women pulled their hoods and veils off.

"RIGHT," shouted man who had come from the rear, "put them fucking back on, NOW!"

"Okay, girls," said Bob in a soft voice, "you're safe, just come with us." Out of the inside of his old grey jacket that he was wearing the man pulled out a long knife and pointed it at Bob and with the market now silent said.

"I have many friends here, for poke your nose in, I take that bitch," he pointed at Sam, "now what the fuck you say English?" Sam turned in the direction of Bert, who was in a light-coloured suit with an open neck blue shirt on, who stood at the next stall, and waved both her arms at him in the air. Bert took a whistle out of his pocket and blew it as loud as he could, to the point some people near him put their hands over their ears. From a nearby car park the rear doors of a parked lorry flew open, and twenty soldiers armed with assault rifles jumped out and ran to the aid of Sam, Bob and the three females, and pointed the rifles at the two men.

"We have many friends here too," Bob smiled to the man, "now what the fuck you say?" The reply was short and to the point.

"Oh fuck!"

*

"Oh, that's lovely," Annabel reported as she sat in a leather armchair in a lounge at the embassy sipping a glass of gin and tonic with Bob and Sam sat on a leather settee facing her, she held the glass up and looked at it. "I have to say there was a time when I thought I would never have one of these again, thank you both so much, I can't believe I' am out." They both smiled.

"You will be home on Tuesday," put in Bob.

"Oh, I really can't wait, this has been absolutely awful, I hope those bastards go away for a very long time. Do you know where the other two girls are?"

"Yes, they are both French, and have been taken to their embassy."

"I only saw them once a week, when we were taken to the market, we were never allowed to talk to each other, the rest of the time we were on our own in rooms, until the men came. I did hear screams." Sam put her hand over her mouth. "I tried to talk to them as we were about to go out once, and got a punch in the mouth by Hamid, the chap who pulled the knife on you Bob, he's a nasty piece of work."

"Your safe now Annabel," smiled Bob as he sipped on a glass of beer, "we are just so pleased we were able to help you." Sam held his hand.

"I just can't say thank you enough, every time I saw you in the market I felt I had hope, sorry for keep walking into you Sam, but when I saw you it was the only way I could think of getting your attention."

"It's fine Annabel, we are just so pleased you are free."

"Are you two married?" she asked the pair on the settee. Before Annabel got an answer, Bert entered the room and sat in another armchair facing them.

"Well," he said with a smile on his face, "we hit the jackpot there, the officer in charge has just called me, they raided the house and it's an Aladdin's cave. They found loads of stolen goods. At the rear of the property were custom made cars and building site diggers, which had been stolen in Europe and brought over here to sell, they had drugs, weapons, guns, thousands upon thousands of pounds in foreign currency, and a massive amount of sterling which they would have used to buy a lot of these things with. Of course, as you know it is illegal here to change money up anywhere else other than a bank."

The pair on the settee each gave a sheepish smile and nodded their heads in agreement.

*

On the morning that the pair were leaving the country Sam talked Bob into going to see Fabi for the last time, "Sam, we saw her yesterday." The previous day they had gone to the orphanage with sweets and toys for the children and had a very tearful farewell with Fabi and Anya after they had taken many photographs.

"I know, but just one last time please, please?" She pleaded

"Oh, you're a nightmare, we will have to make it quick."

"In and out, I promise."

It was a reluctant, "yes," but agree he did.

It was not Anya who answered the door when they arrived at the orphange but one of her assistants who Sam spoke to in French, as she got the reply she put her hand to her mouth then started crying.

"What is it?" Asked Bob.

"She's gone."

"What do you mean, she's gone?"

"A couple came after we were here yesterday and adopted her, after we had gone. Anya has taken her to their home this morning." She grabbed and hugged Bob as she cried.

"Look," he pulled her away from him, "that's what you wanted, we wanted, isn't it, for her to have a family?"

"Yes, of course, but, oh, no your right, we should be pleased and happy for her, she is getting a home, come on," she wiped her face, "we have a plane to catch."

The pair returned to the base camp to hand over their van and say their goodbyes to all the staff in the compound before they were taken to the airport in a mini bus, where they had agreed to meet Bert and Annabel for the afternoon flight to London.

They hugged and shook hands with the cooks, chefs, cleaners who they had become friends with over the past fourteen months. The day before the pair had given the local people their old clothes etc, that they would not be taking home and brought lots of small gifts, mainly sweets to give them.

Sam lastly talked to Zaza. When they were in the minibus Bob asked.

"How's things with Zaza?"

"Well, her husband turned up at the house last night and stormed in."

"Oh no, is she okay?"

"Her father chased him out of the house with the shotgun, and when he was running down the street her Dad fired it in the air above his head, and other people came out of their houses and shouted and threw stones at him. Zaza has lived there since she was a child, they don't think he will be back again."

"Well done Miss Crisp, you did well there, and with Annabel."

"I am very pleased with all that, just upset that we will never see Fabi again, but she has a family now, so I am pleased for her." Bob squeezed her hand as she smiled through her tears.

*

"Where are they?" Asked Sam, "we are going to have to go through passport control soon Bob, you said they would be here."

"They will be here soon, I talked to Bert this morning, everything is fine," came the reply.

"Oh, I just really want us to go home with Annabel, oh look, here's Annabel now," pointed Sam, as the female came through the main doors carrying two suitcases. "Fabi!" Cried Sam as she appeared waving in a wheelchair being pushed by Bert with Anya beside him, Sam ran over and hugged her. "What's going on?"

"Your boyfriend, has adopted Fabi, she is going home with you," replied Bert.

"What?" She stood up, "what's, what's happening?"

"Bob has been setting it up for months and months," came the reply.

"You bugger," she thumped him on the arm as he joined her, "how did you do it?"

"The work at the embassy for the lad's, the paperwork was all for Fabi."

"I don't know what to say," she put her hand to her mouth and started crying. "Oh, I have so many questions?"

Bob hugged her, "we have lots to sort out, but there's nothing you and I can't do Miss Crisp."

"I know, I just, I just can't believe it, it's like all my birthdays and Christmases have all come at once, I am just so happy."

"Here's all of the documents Bob, her name is now Fabi English," Bert handed a brown A4 envelope to Bob containing a passport, exit visa and adoption papers.

"And," Bob continued, "she now has a date of birth, they think she was born in 1980 and her birthday is now the third of December."

"The day after mine," cried Sam.

"Yes, so we can have two days of celebrations for the both of you."

"Oh, my word," cried Sam, "you have actually done it, this is real?" Sam held her mouth again.

"Miss Sam, Mr Bob said I can call him Daddy, and he said to ask if I can call you Mummy, please?"

Sam dropped to her knees in front of Fabi, and said, "yes, yes, yes!" With tears pouring from her eyes.

"There's one last thing," said Annabel as she moved in closer. She nodded to Bob, who went down on one knee in front of Sam and Fabi then took a box out of his pocket, opened it to show a gold and diamond engagement ring, and a piece of paper which he unfolded, then began to read.

We met many miles for here, some time ago,
It was when, I did feel so low.

But across all those miles,
You came and made me smile.

Many problems we had to face,
But we joined together, at times it was like a race.

But as a team we became hard to beat,
There were hard times, but mostly we landed on our feet.

We became so close, like wearing a glove,
It's so good to feel that we share such love.

As I fall on to one knee,
I ask Miss Crisp; will you marry me?"

"Yes, I will Mr English, and I will be Fabi's Mummy and you her Daddy, I have never been so happy in all my life." The three hugged on the ground.

*

The End.

Milton Keynes UK
Ingram Content Group UK Ltd.
UKHW030015010324
438562UK00014B/430